"Looks like you need help," said a rumbling baritone from behind her.

Could the morning get any worse?

"Oh no, I'm fine," Ava said.

"Fine, huh? Aren't those your car keys inside the car?"

"I believe so."

Brice studied her for a moment. "Hey, it's no big deal. This kind of thing happens, right?" Tender feelings came to life and he couldn't seem to stop them. Maybe Ava's keys getting locked inside the car was providential. Just like the fact that he was here to help at just the right moment.

"Let me help. It'll just take a minute, and then you can be on your way," he added.

Why was her every sense attuned to this man? Ava felt his presence like the bright radiant sun on her back, almost as if she was interested in him. But of course, she couldn't be. And she especially couldn't be falling in love with Brice Donovan.

Books by Jillian Hart

Love Inspired

Heaven Sent #143
*His Hometown Girl #180
A Love Worth Waiting For #203
Heaven Knows #212
*The Sweetest Gift #243
*Heart and Soul #251
*Almost Heaven #260
*Holiday Homecoming #272
*Sweet Blessings #295
For the Twins' Sake #308
*Heaven's Touch #315
*Blessed Vows #327
*A Handful of Heaven #335
*A Soldier for Christmas #367
*Precious Blessings #383
*Every Kind of Heaven #387

*The McKaslin Clan

JILLIAN HART

makes her home in Washington State, where she has lived most of her life. When Jillian is not hard at work on her next story, she loves to read, go to lunch with her friends and spend quiet evenings with her family.

Jillian Hart
Every Kind of Heaven

Steeple Hill®

Published by Steeple Hill Books™

STEEPLE HILL BOOKS

Steeple
Hill®

ISBN-13: 978-0-373-87423-1
ISBN-10:   0-373-87423-5

EVERY KIND OF HEAVEN

www.SteepleHill.com

Printed in U.S.A.

I consider that our present sufferings
are not worth comparing with the glory
that will be revealed in us.
—*Romans* 8:18

Chapter One

Baker Ava McKaslin stopped humming as she stepped back from the worktable to inspect the wedding cake. Her footsteps echoed in the industrial kitchen, nearly empty except for a few basics—the sink, countertops and the few pieces of equipment she'd managed to buy off the previous tenant. They'd considered it too cumbersome and expensive to move the industrial oven and fridge, which was just her luck.

She might not have the bakery of her dreams *yet,* God willing, but it was a start. Besides, her cake was spectacular, if she did say so herself.

But what was with all the silence? She cut a look to the long stretch of metal counter behind her. The CD had come to an end. She'd probably forgotten to hit Repeat again. Okay, she forgot most things most of the time. Since her hands were all frosting coated, she hit the Play button with her elbow. The first beats of percussion got her right back into the creative mode. Although some people found it hard to think with bass blasting from her portable boom box, she thought it helped her brain cells to fire…or synapse…or do whatever brain cells did.

As the Christian music pulsed with an upbeat rhythm, she went back to work on the top tier. The delicate scrollwork took patience, not to mention stamina. Her wrist and arms were killing her, since she'd been at this for six hours straight. Ah, the price of being a baker. She ignored the burn in her exhausted muscles. Pain, that didn't matter. What mattered was *not* failing.

Before she'd bought this place, she'd been unofficially in business by using her oldest sister Katherine's snazzy kitchen off and on for a few months. This was her very first wedding cake in her own bakery. How great was that? And it was actually going well—a total shocker. So far there were no disasters. No kitchen fires. No last-minute cancellation of the wedding. It was almost as if this business venture of hers was meant to be.

Maybe she hadn't made a disastrous mistake by jumping into this entrepreneurial thing with both feet. And, best of all, the remodeling contractor would start work soon transforming this drab commercial space into a cheerful bakery shop in less than a couple of weeks. That was another reason why she was in such a great mood.

"Hello?" a man's voice—a stranger's voice—yelled over the booming music.

She screamed. The spatula slipped from her grip. What was a man doing in her kitchen? A man she'd never seen before. Her brain scrambled and her body refused to move. She could only gape at him in wide-eyed horror.

Oh, no. What if he was the backdoor burglar? The thief that had been breaking into the back doors of restaurants and assaulting and stealing? What if this dude was him?

It would be smart to call 9-1-1, but she had no idea where her cell was. There was no business phone installed yet. Even if she did have her cell or a working landline, it wouldn't matter since she was paralyzed in place.

"Uh…uh…" That was the best speech she could manage? Get it together, Ava. You're about to be robbed. "I've seen your face, so I can identify you in a lineup."

The burglar stared at her. Wow, he was really handsome. And he looked startled. His strong, chiseled jaw was clenched tight in, perhaps, fury and his striking dark eyes glittered with viciousness…or maybe that was humor. The left corner of his mouth quirked up as if he were holding back a grin.

Great, she had to get an easily amused thief.

"I've got two bucks in my purse. That's it, buddy. There's not another cent on the premises. You've picked the wrong place to rob. So t-t-turn around r-right now and go away. Go on. Shoo."

There, that ought to scare him off *or* confuse him. She really didn't care which. Adrenaline—or maybe it was terror—started to spill like ice into her veins.

"Go ahead, call the cops." He called her bluff, crossing his arms over his wide chest. He had the audacity to lean one big shoulder against the doorframe, as if he had all the time in the world. He looked more like a movie star than a criminal. "Explain to the police how you left the front door unlocked."

"No, I—" Wait, she *did* forget to lock stuff. And if he'd come in the *front* door, then he wasn't the backdoor thief. Maybe. Unless he'd changed his M.O. and was that very likely? She didn't think so. "I did leave the door unlocked, didn't I?"

"Anyone could walk right in. Even the backdoor burglar. That's who you thought I was, right?"

Okay, her mind was starting to unscramble. He didn't look like any criminal she'd seen on TV. To make matters worse, he looked *better* than any man she'd seen on TV. He was handsome to a fault. His thick black hair fell with disregard for convention over his collar. He wore a short-sleeve polo shirt—black—with the little expensive insignia. His clothes—including his baggy khaki shorts and exclusive manly leather sandals—were top of the line. Expensive.

It was likely that the backdoor thief didn't dress like that or have such a perfect smile. She hit Pause on the boom box. "Okay, I feel dumb now. What were you doing surprising me like that? You just can't go walking into any place you want."

"I'm looking for you, Ava McKaslin." His grin broadened enough to show off a double set of dimples.

Oops. This must be about business, and mistaking a potential customer for a burglar was so not professional. "You've come with a cake order, haven't you, and after meeting me, you've changed your mind."

"No, but it's tempting." The sets of dimples dug deeper as his grin widened. "I've been sent to check on the cake."

"Chloe's cake?" Oh, no. That can't be good. Suddenly her great mood tumbled. "Has she called off her wedding?"

"Nope."

"Changed her mind and eloped?"

"Not to my knowledge."

"Has she gone with another baker and forgot to tell me? Has she postponed the wedding?"

"Let me guess. You're more of a glass-is-half-empty kind of girl, aren't you?"

"Hey, disasters happen. I'm a realist."

Ava knelt to retrieve the spatula. She tossed it into the sink and washed her hands, turning her back to the guy. He wasn't a burglar. She'd leapt to a wrong conclusion, but his being a thief might be better because he'd come with bad news. She knew, although he had yet to admit it, that he'd come to cancel the first cake she'd made in her bakery.

Total doom.

She grabbed a paper towel to dry her hands. "Tell Chloe I appreciate that she went with me, even if it didn't work out. Is she all right?"

"I hope so, since she's getting married tomorrow."

"The wedding's still on?"

"Sure it is."

She was as cute as he remembered. Brice Donovan took a step closer, trying to act like he wasn't stunned. He'd never met any woman who looked so funny and gorgeous all in the same moment. It was the eyes. Those big violet-blue eyes filled with one hundred percent vibrant emotion. They radiated such heart and spirit that he was sucked right in, like being caught in the vortex of a black hole.

It ought to be terrifying, but he didn't mind it so much. He was glad to see her again. She didn't seem to remember seeing him at Chloe's wedding shower, considering she'd mistaken him for a burglar. But he sure remembered her. How could he not? She was unforgettable.

And absolutely adorable. Not that he could see much of her; she was standing behind the most unusual cake he'd ever seen. One large heart-shaped layer was stacked off-center on another, and another over that. Satin-textured, smooth ivory frosting adorned with amazing gold lace and ribbons of some kind of frosting, and colorful sugar flowers everywhere.

Unlike her cake, the designer wasn't as perfectly arranged. She had globs of icing all over her. A streak on her cheek, a dried crown of it in her light blond hair, which was neatly tied back, and a blob just above the tip of her cute little nose.

When he'd agreed to check on the cake's progress for his sister, he'd thought the address was familiar. He knew why the instant he'd pulled into the lot. His construction company had won the bid for renovation—starting next week. The moment he'd spotted the shop's proprietor hard at work, he'd known why Chloe had sent him. She was meddlesome, but then a guy had to tolerate that from his baby sister. Not that he wasn't grateful.

Over the past year, he'd noticed Ava McKaslin around town a couple of times. They didn't belong to the same social circle or church, and didn't live in the same parts of town, so he'd never had an opportunity to talk to her before. There was something about her that always made him smile. Just like he was doing now.

"I've been sent to make sure the cake is on schedule." He stalked forward, wanting to get closer to that smile of hers. "It looks on schedule to me."

"I'll need thirty minutes tops, and then it's done. Chloe doesn't have to worry about a thing. I'll deliver it bright and early at the country club, just as I promised, no sweat."

"She'll be thrilled." He splayed both hands on

the table and leaned toward her, drawn by those eyes, by everything.

Up close, there was nothing artificial about her. She was radiant. She had a fresh-faced complexion and dazzling beauty, sure, but she was unique. She was like the light refracting off a flawless diamond. Hers was a brilliance that was impossible to touch or to capture.

He'd really like to get to know her. "You said you've got thirty minutes until you're done?"

"I promise. You and Chloe have nothing to worry about. Your wedding cake will be perfect." Ava crossed her heart like a girl scout, as cute as a button.

Captivated, Brice felt blinded in a way he'd never been before. He definitely would like to see what this violet-eyed, flawless Ava was really like. He took in the little gold cross at her throat and the sweet way she looked. What was such a good, amazing woman doing single?

She scooped a short spatula into a stainless steel bowl, fluffy with snow-white frosting. "Did you want to come back when I'm done?"

"I'd rather stay, if you don't mind."

"Stay? You don't want to do that. You'd be bored."

"I doubt that. I could watch you work. I've never seen anything like this. It's beautiful, the work you do." He took a breath. Gathered his courage. "If you don't mind, when you're done, we could talk, just you and me."

Ava stared over the top frills of the cake. She

blinked hard, as if she were trying to bring him into focus. Or make sense of what he was saying. "Talk?"

"Sure. We've met before, don't you remember? Maybe we can go down the street for a cup of coffee. Get to know each other better."

"What?" The spatula dropped from her supple artist's fingers and clattered on the metal tabletop. "You want to get to know me *better?*"

Uh-oh. She didn't look happy about that. He'd never had that reaction from a woman before. Okay, maybe he'd jumped the gun. "Do you have a boyfriend? I should have asked first. I noticed you weren't wearing a wedding ring and I assumed—"

She cut him off, circling around the table like a five-star army general. "You *assumed?* What's wrong with you?"

He couldn't believe how mad she looked. "Hey, what did I do? I just wanted to talk."

"Talk? Oh, is that what men like you call it? You need to get some morals."

Well, at least she was a lady with serious principles. He liked that. He respected Ava's inner fiber. It was a little passionate, but he liked that, too. He held up both hands, a show of surrender. "Hey, I didn't know you were attached. Why wouldn't you be? Look at you. Of course you have a boyfriend. He probably worships at your feet."

"No I don't have a boyfriend, but what about you and Chloe? You're getting married! You should leave. Go."

Normally, he might take offense at her dismissal, but he didn't seem to mind.

No boyfriend, huh? Okay, call him interested. No, call him dazzled, that's what he was. She fascinated him, all pure inner fire and feeling. But this wasn't going well. Usually he got a better response than this.

"What am I going to have to tell your bride?" Her sweetheart-shaped face turned pink with fury. "The poor woman thinks she's getting married to Mr. Right. Little does she know you're Mr. Yuck, wanting to get to know me the evening before your wedding. I don't think you want to chat, either!"

So, that was it. Whew. For a minute there, he was afraid she really didn't like him. "You misunderstood."

"Misunderstood? Oh, I don't think so."

Men, Ava fumed. What was wrong with the species? *This* was why she wasn't married. Too many of the gender were just like this guy, and nothing made her madder. Spitting mad. "I'm a good Christian girl. Get a clue, buddy. Are you misunderstanding me now?"

"Uh, no. I noticed the gold cross. You look like a very nice Christian girl to me."

He was being agreeable now, but it didn't matter. "Poor Chloe. Now what do I do? Do I tell her? Or do I make you do it? A man like you doesn't deserve a nice wife like her. What kind of man would do that to the woman he was about to marry?"

He chuckled. Actually chuckled, the sound rich as cream. His dimples deepened. Tiny, attractive laugh lines crinkled around his kind, warm brown eyes.

That was the problem. He didn't look like a cheater. He looked like a nice guy. What did a girl do in a world where icky men could look as good as the nice ones?

She'd had this problem before. This is why she had a newly instated policy of staying away from every last one of them, unless they needed to buy a cake from her, of course. She intended to stick to her current no-man policy one hundred percent. "This is the last time I'm telling you to leave."

"Okay, stand down soldier." He held up both hands as if he were surrendering. "I'll go. But please accept my apology. I'm sorry. I don't know what I was thinking."

"Obviously you weren't thinking at all. Or you thought that I looked easy, and let me tell you, you couldn't be more wrong."

"Ava McKaslin, you look like class to me. I can't help noticing that you aren't happy with my interest."

"You got that right. Hey! You're not heading toward the door."

"We're not done discussing the cake." He had the audacity to grin again.

That grin became more charming each time he used it, Ava thought, making him look like the absolute perfect guy.

She'd been fooled by dimples and charm too many times before. "The cake will be ready and delivered at the country club's service entrance by nine tomorrow morning, as agreed. There. Discussion done."

"Chloe will be relieved. You aren't going to mention this little misunderstanding to her, right?"

Didn't that take the prize? "I don't know. I may have to consult my sisters and my minister on this one. She should know the kind of man she's marrying."

"I'm not the groom."

"Oh, *sure* you're not." Ava rolled her eyes. Some men would resort to anything. Men like him had made her give up dating. Perhaps forever. Good thing she'd vowed to turn all her energy to making a success of her business, because it would be impossible to make marriage work considering the men running around these days.

She reloaded her spatula with frosting. "You're not gone yet."

He sighed, resigned as he backed through the kitchen doorway. "I guess I'll see you at the wedding, huh?"

"Not if I can help it." Really, what gave this guy the idea that she was interested? "I'd better follow you to the door to make sure you really leave. Then I'm going to lock it, so no more riffraff can get in."

"At least I'm not the backdoor burglar, or you would have really been in trouble. That spatula loaded with frosting wouldn't be much of a weapon against a revolver." He paused in the front door, framed by the brilliant June sunshine. His grin went cosmic. "By the way, you have frosting on your nose. It's cute. Real cute."

"You're not so attractive, Mr. Yuck."

"Ava, listen. I'm *not* the groom. When you deliver the cake, stick around for the wedding. You'll see I'm the best man. So, how about it?"

She grabbed his arm and gave him a shove. It was impossible not to notice he felt like solid steel. Once he'd rocked backwards a step, she was able to slam the door. Not that he was harmful, she thought as she threw the deadbolt, but she'd had enough of not-so-stellar men.

So why did she gravitate to the front windows that gave her a perfect view of the parking lot?

Because she wanted to make sure he left, the horrible man, trying to pick up a woman on the night before his wedding. Despicable.

It was hard to believe a human being was capable of behaving so badly, but she'd been propositioned like that before. Three wedding cakes ago. Darrin Fullerton had thought that when she delivered the two-tier caramel coconut cake that she was ready to serve up something else, too. It still shocked her. Too many men needed to spend more time reading their Bibles. Filling their minds with uplifting and spiritual subjects. Learning to recite the Psalms. List the seven deadly sins. That kind of thing.

The groom climbed into a bright red luxury sports car—not surprising—and zipped away. As he passed by the shop's glassed front, his driver's side window whipped down and he lifted his designer aviator sunglasses to give her a wink.

Horrible. Anger turned her vision to pure crimson. Seconds passed until she could see normally again. The parking lot was empty, the red sports car long gone.

Her cell phone chimed. The cheerful jingle came from very near. She looked down and found it in her apron pocket. The display said it was her twin sister, Aubrey. "Howdy."

"I'm just pulling up into the lot. I can see your frowny face from here."

"I have more than a frowny face on. It's my down-on-men face."

"Wow. What happened?"

"Oh, another groom trying to get one last party in before he commits." Ava spotted her bright yellow SUV cautiously creeping across the empty lot. Her sister had borrowed it and was coming closer. "What is it with men and commitment? I don't get why it's so terrifying. It's not any more frightening than a lot of things. Like premature baldness."

"Crow's feet."

"New car payments. Now *that's* scary. Which is why I'm glad I've given up on dating. Who cares if I ever get married?"

"*You* do."

"Too true." Ava sighed. "I've got a few more minutes to finish up, and then I'm good to go."

Aubrey brought the vehicle to a slow stop at the curb outside the window. She leaned forward, squinting through the windshield. "You brought a change of clothes, right? Or are you going to the movies like that?"

"I knew I forgot something." Ava snapped the phone shut. Who needed a man when she had enough disaster in her life?

Too bad the kind of man she needed—perfect in every way, no selfishness, no flaws or questionable morals—didn't exist.

So what was a nice girl to do? Settle for Mr. So-So or Marginally Moral? As if!

Ava unlocked the door for Aubrey and went back to work. There was the wedding cake in all its love-liness, fresh and beautiful like the new promise a wedding should be. But would she ever know what that new promising love felt like? No.

Disappointed, she grabbed a clean spatula from the drawer by the sink and went back to work, making sugar roses. Trying not to dwell on the sadness that was buried so deep inside she could *almost* pretend it didn't exist. She didn't want to live her life without knowing true love.

But with the men she kept running into, she had no other choice.

Chapter Two

The next morning, Brice pulled into the country club's parking lot and killed the engine. It was 8:53 a.m. Hadn't Ava promised the cake would be delivered by nine?

He climbed out into the hot sunshine, made hotter by the monkey suit he had to wear. He hooked a finger beneath his tie and tugged until he had a little more breathing room. After remoting the door locks, he hadn't gone five steps before his cell rang. He thumbed it from his pocket. Seeing his sister's number on the call screen made his step lighter. "Having cold feet yet?"

"No way. I can't wait to get married. I don't have a single doubt. Where are you?"

"Where do you think?"

"Ha! You're up to something. You're not answering me." She sounded happy, her voice light and easy.

Brice was glad for his little sister. He wouldn't mind having that kind of happiness in his life. He checked his Rolex. Another minute had ticked by. He shouldered through the club's main door. "Where I am is none of your business. Is Mom giving you problems?"

"When isn't she giving me problems? She means well. At least, that's what I keep telling myself so I don't flip out. She's made two of my bridesmaids cry. She's decided the wedding planner isn't capable and is trying to take over."

"Do you need me to come run interference?"

"Do you know what I need you to do?" Chloe sounded as if she was very glad he'd asked. "I'd love it if you could swing by the club and check on the cake."

I know what you're up to little sister, he thought. But he didn't mind. He hadn't been able to stop thinking of Ava since he'd left her shop yesterday.

It ate at him that she thought he was the groom. She was right—from her mistaken perspective he did look like a Mr. Yuck. Now, that was a misperception he had to change, even if he had to show her two forms of ID to do it.

Because he didn't want to encourage his sister, he tried to sound indifferent. Not at all interested. "Tell me what you know about this baker you went with."

"Ha! You like her. I know you do."

"I don't know her." *Yet.* But he intended to change that.

As he began looking around the room, he spotted her through the closed French doors into the ballroom and he froze in place. Ava. Seeing her was like the first light of dawn rising, and that was something he'd never felt before. *Ever.*

"I met Ava when we were volunteering at the community church's shelter kitchen." Chloe sounded very far away, although the cell connection was crystal clear. "She's sweet and kind and hysterical. We had a great time, until they asked her to leave."

What had she said? Brice's mind was spinning. He couldn't seem to focus. All he could think of was Ava. Her thick, shiny hair was tied up into a haphazard ponytail, bouncing in time with her movements. She was busily going over the cake, checking each colorful flower and sparkling golden accent.

She hadn't noticed him yet and seemed lost in her own world. She had a set of ear buds in, probably listening to a pocket-sized digital music player. She wore jeans and a yellow T-shirt that said on the back "Every Kind of Heaven" in white script.

Was the saying true? It had to be. She *did* look like everything sweet and good in the world.

"Brice? Are you listening to me?"

He felt dazed, as if he'd been run over by a bus. He couldn't orient himself in place and time. Any minute Ava would look up, and when she saw him, she'd leap to the same conclusion as before—that he was Mr. Yuck. If he didn't act quickly, would she start lobbing frosting at him?

He'd never quite had that affect on a woman before.

"Look, Chloe. I gotta go. Call if you need anything, okay?"

"Sure. You'll make sure Ava doesn't need any help, right? She's just starting her business and she hasn't hired anyone yet. She'll need some assistance with all the favors we ordered. Remember, if you change your mind and decide to bring a date to my wedding, feel free."

"Sure. Right," he said vaguely.

Ava. He was having the toughest time concentrating on anything else. His thoughts kept drifting to the woman on the other side of the door.

When he opened it, he heard a lightly muttered, "Oops!"

Ava's voice made his senses spin.

Think, Brice. He clicked off his phone and stepped into the ballroom.

Morning light spilled through the long row of closed French doors and onto her. She looked tinier than he remembered. Maybe it was that she had such a big personality that she gave the impression of stature. She was surprisingly petite with slender lines and almost skinny arms and legs. There was no one else helping. How she'd delivered that big cake by herself was a mystery. It had to be heavy.

He knew the moment she sensed his presence. The line of her slender shoulders stiffened. Every muscle went completely rigid. She pulled the ear buds out of her ears, turning toward him in one swift movement.

"You." If looks could kill, he'd at least be bleeding. "What are you doing here? You're just like Darrin Fullerton. He showed up when I was delivering the cake to beg me not to say anything to his bride. He'd been drunk, he'd said, and didn't know what he was doing when he propositioned me. As if that's any excuse!"

Quick, Brice, look innocent. He held up both hands in surrender. "Wait. I'm nothing like that Fullerton guy. I'm a completely innocent best man. Really."

"Innocent? I don't think so."

Ava gave him her best squinty-eyed look. He was bigger than she remembered, a good six feet tall. When she'd shoved him out the door of her bakery, it had been like trying to move a bulldozer.

She went up on tiptoe so she could glare at him directly, not exactly eye to eye, but it was the best she could manage, being so short. "Are you ashamed of yourself? At all?"

He didn't look unashamed. "Chloe's going to love that cake. You did an amazing job."

"Now if only I can control the urge to lob the top tier at you."

"Do you think you can restrain that urge for a few seconds? I've got something to show you." He reached into his back pocket.

Men were much more trouble than they were worth, she concluded. But why did he have to have such an amazing grin? That's probably what Chloe saw in him; it obviously blinded her to all his multitude of faults. Poor Chloe. "You should be getting ready for your wedding, but what are you doing? Trying to get me not to tell—"

He flashed a card at her. "This ought to clear up the confusion."

"I'm not the one who's confused. You owe me an apology and your bride an enormous apology and—"

He waved the card in front of her. "Look closer."

She squinted to bring the card into focus. Not a card. It was a driver's license. Some of her fury sagged as she realized the picture, which was, of course, perfect, matched the man standing before her. The name to the left of the photo was Brice Donovan.

What? Her mind screeched to a sudden halt. She sank back onto her heels, staring, feeling her jaw drop. Brice Donovan. Chloe Donovan's *brother.* Not the groom.

"I'm the best man," he said, wagging the card. "Do you finally believe me?"

His eyes darkened with amusement, but they weren't unkind. No, not at all. A strong warmth radiated from him as he leaned close, and then closer.

That thought spun around in her brain for a moment, like a car's engine stuck in neutral. Then it hit her. She'd insulted, yelled at and accused a perfectly innocent man.

It was hard to know just what to say. Talk about being embarrassed. Had she really said all those things to him? She felt faint. Wasn't he on the city's most eligible bachelor's list? It was just in last weekend's paper. She couldn't believe she hadn't recognized him.

Why did these things always happen to her? She clipped her case closed. He was probably waiting for an apology. An apology for the accusations. The fact that she'd been beyond rude to him, one of the wealthiest men from one of the most prominent families in Montana.

Lovely. Her face heated from the humiliation starting to seep into her soul. "Oops. My bad."

"You think?" He crooked one brow, amusement softening the impressive impact of all iron-solid six feet of him.

The effect was scrambling her brain cells, and that wasn't helping her to think.

"Chloe's going to really love what you've done with this cake." He jammed his hands into his pockets, looking like a cover model come to life. "It's going to make her so happy. Thank you."

Now what did she say? She'd been awful to him and he was complimenting the cake she'd worked so hard on. It made her feel even worse. "I'm trying to figure out how to apologize, but *sorry* seems like too small a word."

"Don't even worry about it."

"Thanks," she said shyly.

Brice Donovan's smile made her even more muddled. Before he'd walked into the ballroom she'd been so happy, thinking how pleased Chloe was going to be. But now? Her heart twisted with agony. Her face was so hot and red from embarrassment, she could feel her skin glow. What she could see of her nose was as bright as a strawberry.

This was no way for a professional baker to behave. Feeling two inches tall, she looked up to Brice's kind eyes. He wasn't laughing at her. No. That was one saving grace, right?

"I am sorry. Really. Tell Chloe best wishes. This cake is my gift to her."

"But she hired you to bake it."

"So she thinks. I've got to go, I have another project to work on, but this, the groom's cake and the favors, it's all from me to her. She was a good friend to me when I really needed one." Her chest felt so tight, she felt ready to burst. Embarrassment had turned into a horrible, sharp pain right behind her sternum.

Doom. She'd just made a mess of this. Would there ever be one time—just *once*—when she didn't make a mess of something? There was no way to fix this, and the cake was finished. There was nothing else to do but grab her case and her baseball cap.

Somehow she managed to speak without strangling on her embarrassment. "Goodbye, Mr. Donovan. And I am s-sorry again."

"Wait, don't go yet, I—"

"I have to." She was already walking away. She had work waiting and she couldn't face him a second longer. She'd humiliated herself enough for one day and it was only 9:15 a.m. She hadn't even had breakfast yet. Way to go, Ava.

She wasn't aware of crossing the room, only that she was suddenly at the kitchen. But she was aware of him. Of his presence behind her in the spill of light through the expansive windows. She didn't have to look at him as she pushed through the kitchen door to know that he was watching her. She could feel the tangible weight of his touch between her shoulder blades. What was he thinking?

Lord, I don't want to know. She kept going. She hit the back service doors and didn't slow until she felt the soothing morning sun on her face.

She skidded to a stop in the gravel and breathed in the fresh morning air. The scents of warm earth and freshly mowed grass calmed her a little. She breathed hard, getting out all the negative feelings. There were a lot of them. And trying not to hear her mother's voice saying, *You wreck everything you touch. Can't you stop making a mess for two seconds?*

She'd been seven, and she could still hear the shrill impatience. She still felt like that little girl who just didn't know how things went wrong no matter how hard she tried.

You're just a big dope, Ava, she told herself. What kind of grown adult had the problems she had? Wasn't she going to turn over a new leaf? Start out right this time? Stop making so many dumb mistakes?

Well, no more. She wasn't going to think about the way she'd embarrassed herself back there. She'd been hoping that by doing a good job with Chloe's cake, she'd get some word-of-mouth interest and her business would naturally pick up.

But after this, what were the chances that anyone was going to remember what the cake looked like?

None. All Brice Donovan was going to do was to talk about the dingbat cake lady who mistook him—the city of Bozeman's golden boy—for a philandering groom.

Her SUV blurred into one bright yellow blob. She blinked hard until her eyes cleared and reached into her pocket for her keys.

The only thing she could do was go on from here. Simply write off this morning as a lesson learned. What else could she do? She reached into her other pocket, but it was empty. No, it couldn't be. Her heart jack hammered. Where were her keys?

She did another search of her pockets. Jeans front pockets. No key. Back pockets. No key. Those were the only pockets she had. Panic began to stutter in her chest. *Where were her keys?*

There. Sitting right in plain view on the rear passenger seat. *Inside* the locked vehicle. Right next to her cell phone and her sunglasses.

Super-duper. What did she do now?

"Looks like you need help," said a rumbling baritone from behind her. A baritone she recognized. Brice Donovan.

Could the morning get any worse? How was she going to save her dignity now—or what was left of it? "H-help? Oh, no, I'm fine."

"Fine, huh? Aren't those your car keys inside the car?"

"I believe so."

"I don't know too many people who can actually lock their keys in the car with a remote. Don't you need the remote to lock the door?"

"Yes." She plopped her baseball cap on her head and pulled the bill low, trying to hide what she could of her face. Her nose was bright red again.

Brice studied her for a moment before realization dawned. Oh, he knew why she was acting this way, shuffling away from him, head down, avoiding his gaze. She was embarrassed. Well, she didn't need to be. "Hey, it's no big deal. This kind of thing happens, right?"

The tension eased from her tight jaw and rigid shoulders. She shrugged helplessly. "I've only had this car for a few months and I haven't figured out all the settings yet. It's too technologically advanced for me."

"I doubt that." Tender feelings came to life and he couldn't seem to stop them. Maybe her keys getting locked inside the car was providential. Just like the fact that he was here to help at just the right moment. "I have a knack for this kind of thing."

"Thanks, but please don't bother."

She still wouldn't look at him. Instead, she stared hard at the toes of her sunshine-yellow sneakers. Yellow, just like her SUV. There was nothing mundane about Ava McKaslin.

He liked that. Very much.

She surprised him by sidestepping away, heading back to the service doors.

"Hey, where are you going?"

"To find a phone."

"To call…?"

"My sister to come with the extra set of keys."

Wow. She really didn't want his help. Getting a woman to like him used to be easier than this, although he *had* been out of the dating circuit for a long time. After all, he'd dated Whitney two years before he'd proposed to her, which had turned out to be a much longer engagement period than either of them had expected. That put him nearly four, no, almost five years out of practice.

But still, he just didn't remember it being so difficult. "Your sister doesn't need to go to the trouble of driving out here. I'll break in for you."

She paused midstride.

He could sense her indecision, so he tried again. "Let me help. It'll take a minute and then you can be on your way."

"But I was so rude to you."

"So? If you're worried about retaliation, forget it. I'm a turn-the-other-cheek kind of guy. And I won't leave a scratch on your new car. Promise."

"And just why does a man like you know how to break into a car without leaving any evidence?"

"Chloe used to lock herself out of her car, too. I need a coat hanger. I'll be right back." He shouldered past her, pausing at the base of the concrete steps.

Why was her every sense attuned to this man? She felt Brice's presence like the bright radiant sun on her back, almost as if she was interested in him, but, of course, she couldn't be. She was done with thinking about any guy, and done with dreams of falling in love.

She was done with dreams like Brice Donovan.

Chapter Three

"Mission accomplished. No trouble at all."

His voice moved through Ava like a warm breeze. She turned toward him as her car's alarm went off. While the vehicle honked and the headlights flashed, he calmly opened the back door, grabbed the key ring with the remote and pressed the button. The horn silenced, the headlights died.

For him, it had been simple. But for her? She'd had to stand here and watch him, knowing he was helping her out of sympathy. Because he'd felt pity for his little sister's friend.

She would rather fall through a big black hole in the ground than to have to look Brice Donovan in the eye one more time. Sure, he was being gallant and incredibly nice, but it wasn't as if she could erase the things she'd said to him. She heard all the adjectives she'd called him roll around in her head.

Mr. Yuck. Riffraff. She'd told him to *get some morals.* How could she have not recognized him? How could she have made such a mistake?

"All done. And without any damage, thanks to the caterer." He finished bending a wire hanger back into place, but his gaze seared her from six feet away. "Lucky for us she had this in her van."

"Yep, lucky for us." But she didn't feel fortunate. Her nose was still strawberry red, but now it felt hot, too, as if it were glowing under its own energy source.

He opened her driver's side door, looking every inch the handsome millionaire in the designer tux he wore, which fit him like a vision. Of course. He appeared every inch the proverbial prince. And suddenly she knew how Cinderella felt in her ragged dress, wishing she could put on a fancy dress and change her circumstances.

"Here are your keys." They rested on his wide, capable palm.

She couldn't help but notice how strong his hand was. Calluses roughened his skin, as if he worked hard for a living. But that couldn't be. Wasn't he a trust fund kind of guy?

"Thanks, again."

It took all her willpower to meet his gaze. His eyes were so kind and tender. Clearly, he wasn't holding the mistaken identity thing against her. What a relief.

"Goodbye, Brice." She scooped the keys from

his hand as quickly as she could, but her fingertips brushed his hand.

It was like touching a piece of heaven. A corner of serenity. The shame within her faded until there was only a hush in her soul. She didn't know why this happened, but it couldn't be a good sign. She hopped into her car, grabbed her belt as Brice closed her door. Their gazes met, held through the tempered glass, and her world stilled. Her heart forgot to beat.

Probably from the aftereffects of a lethal dose of embarrassment and nothing else—surely not interest, she told herself as she started the engine. But she knew, down deep, that wasn't the truth. The truth wasn't something she could examine too closely.

She drove away, into the sun, purposefully keeping her gaze on the road ahead. She resisted the urge to peek at her rearview mirror and see if he was standing there, watching her go.

Chloe had cried in happiness at her first glimpse of the wedding cake. The cake had been cut, pictures taken, and everyone in the ballroom had been served, and still he could hear the conversation buzzing about the unbelievable cake. It had looked like a porcelain creation of art and beauty, impossible that it was edible. But every piece, from the intricate lace ruffles to the golden beads to the delicate curls of rose petals, had tasted as sweet as heaven.

Each of the two hundred carefully stacked

serving boxes, printed to match the lacework of the cake, held an individual cake for the guests to take home. A heart-shaped version with sugary miniature rosebuds and golden ribbons. He thought of the woman who had done so much work as a gift to his sister. Chloe didn't know it yet since he hadn't found the moment to tell her. She looked as happy as a princess in her frosty white gown at her husband's side.

Brice thanked God for his sister's happiness. He wouldn't mind having some of that kind of joy of his own. He took a gulp of sparkling cider, draining the glass. This was the spot where Ava had stood earlier this morning, with the pale morning sunshine sprinkling over her like a blessing.

Then she'd driven away. What had she been thinking? Did she like him at all? She hadn't acted like it, and yet he'd thought he'd glimpsed something in her eyes. Something that made him think she might be feeling this, too.

Then again, she'd driven off pretty fast. That couldn't be the best sign.

"*There* you are, big brother. You've been hiding." Chloe swept close in her cloud of a dress.

"You know me. All this fancy stuff makes me itch."

She slipped her arm through his. "You look dashing. Five of my former sorority sisters asked me if you were seeing someone."

"And you said…?"

"That you seem to be interested in someone. But if I'm wrong, I have a long list of available women I can set you up with, Mr. Most Eligible Bachelor."

"You know I had nothing to do with that. It's not me." That only made him feel more out of place. Like he was a rich playboy looking for a fast lifestyle or a great catch for a debutante—both equally wrong.

All he wanted was to trade in this getup for his favorite T-shirt, jeans and his broken-in work boots. That's who he really was, and all this glam and glitter made his palms sweat. He swept his hand toward the cake. "You don't need to set me up with a date. I can do it myself."

"Would you rather Mom did it? She's working on it, you know. I was just trying to help out."

"I know." If anyone knew how rough of a time he'd had after the breakup with Whitney, it was Chloe. She meant well. "I can handle it from here."

"I never doubted it." She rose up on tiptoe to brush a sisterly kiss to his cheek. "I want you to be happy. I saw how you looked at Ava at my shower."

"Exactly how was that?"

"Like you were glimpsing heaven. Don't worry, I haven't said anything to her, but you should ask her out. I bet she says yes."

"I've tried that, but I don't think she likes me." Like he needed his baby sister's dating advice. He could handle his own love life just fine. "She said no."

"And since when does Brice Donovan take no for

an answer?" She flounced away, grinning over her shoulder at him. "Try again, silly. Look out, here comes Mom."

The problem was, his mother had been dropping some pretty strong hints lately. Now that she had Chloe successfully matched, she must be refocusing her energy on him. She seemed determined as she barreled through the crowd. Flawless, dressed in diamonds and flowing silk, she looked deceptively like a genteel upper-class lady instead of the five-star general she really was.

"Brice. You have been hiding again." She tugged at his tie, unknotted and hanging loose. "This isn't a barnyard. And what are you doing all the way over here? What are people going to think?"

He accepted the china dessert plate a server handed him. "Maybe people will think that I'm having a second piece of cake."

"Yes. The cake. Horrible, that's what it is. I don't know what Chloe was thinking going with that McKaslin girl."

"That she wanted her friend to make her wedding cake."

"Ridiculous. That cake is unsophisticated and completely unacceptable. And the taste of it, why, it's much too sweet. What is wrong with that girl? I told Chloe. I said, you're going to regret going with her."

"Mom, stop. You're doing it again."

"But did she listen to me? No, she had to have

her own way. We ought to have gone with a professional, not some iffy girl who thinks because our family is richer than hers, she has the right to charge us an arm and a leg."

He laid a hand on his mom's arm to stop her. Sometimes she got such a wind going—sort of like gravity's effect on a snowball rolling downhill—that she simply couldn't realize what she was saying. "Chloe's happy, and that's all that matters. Besides, how much did Ava charge?"

"Ava, is it?" Mom's face pinched, something only she could do and still look dignified. "I wouldn't be so familiar with her if I were you. Her family has money, goodness, but that mother of hers."

"People have been known to say the same thing about Chloe." He said it gently, because he knew his mother didn't mean to be harsh. She simply wasn't aware of it. "I think Ava did an amazing job. So does everyone else in the room. Maybe you should learn to like sweet. You're awfully fond of the bitter."

"That had better not be a veiled reference to me, young man." His mom smiled and tried to hide it, but her eyes were twinkling. "I work hard for this reputation. If people aren't afraid of you, they take advantage. Now, come with me and say hello to a few of my dear friends."

"To the *daughters* of your friends, you mean."

"Crystal Frost is back from her disastrous

divorce to that big real estate broker in Seattle. She's perfect for you."

"Perfect? I don't think so." He took a bite of cake, and sweetness flooded his mouth. The frosting was as rich as cream cheese, and the cake was delicious and buttery. *Perfect.*

"Hello, Brice. Excuse me." One of his mother's friends had sauntered over and gestured toward the cake. "Lynn, this is all so lovely. I came to plead for the name of the designer. My Carly must have a cake like this for her wedding."

Brice knew it would probably drain his mother of her life energy to say something kind about anyone. She was his mom, so he tried to save her from herself. And he wanted to help the cute baker, even if she didn't want to have coffee with him. "Ava McKaslin is the designer and I highly recommend her. Chloe loved working with her."

"Oh, let me think which McKaslin girl. Oh, of course. The friend of your sister's. One of the twins?"

"Yep. She has a shop off Cherry Lane. My company starts renovation on it this week."

"I know which shop you mean. Why, thank you, Brice. You do know that my Crystal is back from Seattle. She's here somewhere." Maxime scanned the room. "Where did she go?"

Uh-oh. Time to escape while he could. "I have to go. Mrs. Frost, it was good seeing you again. Bye, Mom."

He left quickly and didn't look back. It wasn't until he hit the foyer that he realized he still had hold of his dessert plate. Ava's cake. As if he couldn't quite let her go.

The only reason Ava heard her cell ring was because of the break between songs. The electronic chime echoed in the silence of her shop's kitchen. She set down her pastry cone, hit the Pause button on her CD player and went in search of her phone.

Not in her apron pocket. Not on the kitchen counter. She followed the electronic ringing to her gym bag. She unzipped the outside compartment and *ta da,* there it was.

As she grabbed her phone, she realized it was after four. Mrs. Carnahan was supposed to drop by for the birthday cake in ten minutes! Good thing it was almost done. Well, it *would* be done if she'd stop fussing. But after this morning's disaster, she wanted this cake to be perfect.

She flipped open the phone. "I'm late, I know. I was supposed to call an hour ago. My bad."

Instead of her sister's sensible response, a man's resonant chuckle vibrated in her ear. "Keeping your boyfriend waiting?"

It took her a moment to place that voice. Brice Donovan. If he was calling, that could only mean one thing. "Chloe wasn't happy with the cake?"

Disappointment drained her and she sank onto the floor next to her gym bag. Not only had she failed at something she'd tried her hardest at, something that she was good at, but she'd let down a friend. "I'm so sorry."

"Now, wait one minute. That's not why I'm calling."

"It's not?"

"No." His voice warmed like melting chocolate, kind and friendly. "I'm calling to thank you. You made her very happy. She didn't want to cut into the cake because it was too pretty."

"Really? Chloe was happy? Whew!" That was a relief. Now, if she could just forget flinging insults, she'd be doing well. Don't even think about what happened, she told herself. Look forward, not back. Don't dwell on what went wrong.

Problem was, that was easier said and not so easy to do. She took a quivering breath. "Good. Then my work is done."

"And your work is?"

"To make this world a sweeter place one cake at a time. I know it's not solving world strife, but it's the only talent I seem to have, so I'm going with it."

"Surely that's not your only gift."

"Uh, you don't want to hear the long list of disasters I've left in my wake. Speaking of which, I have a cake to get ready and box for a client."

"You can't do that and talk to me?"

"If I want to drop the cake. I need two hands."

Don't think of him in that tux, she thought. Or how amazing he looked. Or how kind he'd been when he'd helped her recover her keys. What had he been thinking when she'd driven away? That unreadable expression in his eyes came back to her now and unsettled her. Why?

Just forget it, Ava. Just forget him. "I appreciate the call. Thank you."

"Well, now, I'm not done with you yet."

"Why am I not surprised?" She couldn't keep the curiosity out of her voice. Or the smile. Both the humiliation she'd felt and the failure seemed far away. Maybe it was because she knew this was a pity call. He felt sorry for the dopey cake lady. Face it, he was Mr. Wow, and she was lucky to keep the date and time straight.

That meant this was a business call. How great was that? She hadn't totally embarrassed herself beyond redemption after all. Cool. "Hopefully you're interested in placing an order?"

"You've got a renovation coming up. How are you going to fill your orders?"

He probably knew about the upcoming renovation because Chloe had been the one to recommend a construction company. "I'm planning on using my sister's kitchen. She's spending most of her evenings with her fiancé and his daughter, so I've commandeered her condo."

"Then maybe you and I can talk later. Say, Monday morning, bright and early?"

"Oops. Can't. I have construction dudes coming by bright and early."

"That's a coincidence because I—"

"I'm totally sorry, but my customer is here. Can I call you back and we can make an appointment? I can show you my catalogue and have some samples ready."

"Why don't I come by on Monday sometime?" Brice leaned back in his car seat and could see the bakery's front door over the curve of the side mirror. There was a grandmotherly woman at the front door, waving at Ava through the glass.

"Thanks, Mr. Donovan. I really appreciate this. Bye!" There was a click in his ear.

He slid his sunglasses down his nose to get a better view as the front door swung open and there was Ava, dressed in her jeans and that yellow T-shirt, her hair tied back and her genuine smile bright as she waved her hands, talking away to her customer.

Okay, this isn't how he figured things would go. Again. Ava wasn't going to make this easy for him.

She caught his gaze again, moving back into sight with a cake made like a giant dump truck. The red chassis and the bright blue bed made it look like the real toy. Even from a distance, he could see the details. The driver behind the steering wheel, the big black tires, and real-looking dirt.

When she opened the other box, he watched the grandmother's face brighten a notch. There were what had to be small cake rocks about the size of his thumb in chubby yellow buckets. One for each little guest, he figured.

The grandmother looked delighted. But it was the sight of Ava that drew him, multifaceted and flawless, shining like one perfect jewel. She probably didn't realize how she shone from the inside out when she was happy. How caring she was as she refolded the side panels and tucked the lids of the boxes into place. How she waved away what was probably a compliment with ease. She was like no one he'd ever seen before.

Something happened inside him when he looked at Ava. Something that made his spirit come more alive.

He was going to try again. She was a sparkle he could not resist.

He put the car into gear and started driving. Her cheerful words replayed in his mind. *Hopefully you're interested in placing an order?* She'd sounded so full of joy. How was he going to tell her he hadn't meant he wanted to order a cake, but to talk to her about that cup of coffee he'd mentioned earlier?

And what about the renovation? She'd sounded as if the construction guys who were coming had nothing to do with him and his company. She did know he was a part owner, right?

Then again, Ava might not have noticed. His business partner, Rafe, had handled the contracts and the scheduling, and was supervising this project.

Brice hit the speed dial on his cell and waited for it to connect. He'd see if Rafe wouldn't mind switching jobs. Being around Ava every working day for the next two weeks sounded like a good idea. No, a brilliant idea, considering how much he wanted to get to know her.

How would she take it? He was definitely anxious to see the look on her face when he walked into her shop bright and early Monday morning. What would happen then? Only God knew.

One thing was for sure, it was going to be a whole lot of fun to find out.

"Good news!" Ava announced as she sailed through the front door of their apartment. "Mrs. Carnahan loved the cake. She said her little grandson was going to be so happy. And your idea about adding bonus party favors at no charge—it was brilliant. She loved the little rocks I made."

Her twin, Aubrey poked her head out of the kitchen. "What did I tell you?"

"I know, you're *always* right. I don't deny it." Ava rolled her eyes, shut the door with her foot and dropped her purse, gym bag and keys on the floor. "Instead of takeout burgers, I splurged and got Thai. Cashew chicken, stir-fried rice and that noodle dish you love."

"Well done." Aubrey's smile turned full-fledged as she reached for the big takeout sack. "Hurry up, get changed. I'll get us all set up."

"I'm late, I know. But it was an excellent day despite it all. Who knew?" Ava took off for her bedroom, a total disaster. One day when she got enough time, it would be the epitome of orderliness. But since she wasn't sure when that would be, she had to go with the flow.

Knowing Aubrey was waiting, she tossed her clothes on the floor, kicked her sandals toward the closet and dug around in the laundry basket of clean clothes for her favorite sweatpants and T-shirt. After she found her fuzziest socks, she flew down the little hall.

Aubrey was in the living room setting two heaping plates of food onto two TV trays facing the widescreen TV they couldn't afford but got anyway. Not smart, and her poor credit card was bent from the weight of debt, but it was nice to watch Clark Gable in forty-two-inch glory.

"If you would have remembered to call before I hit the video store, you would have had some say in tonight's movie," Aubrey said as she settled down on the couch.

"Hey, the cell waves work both ways. You could have called me."

"I'm always calling you." Aubrey reached for her napkin and shook it open over her lap. "So, I take it the Donovan cake delivery went well this morning. You haven't mentioned the groom. What happened with that?"

"Oh, that's a disaster. Total doom. You know

me." While she'd told her sister about insulting Brice Donovan, she hadn't given her the day's full update.

"Men." Aubrey shook her head, disapproving. "And to think Chloe's groom, Mark Upton, is supposed to be like last year's most eligible bachelor. Philanthropic. An upstanding Christian. I guess it just shows, you never know about some men. They show one face when they really have another."

"Well, now, that's not exactly the case." Ava slipped behind the TV tray and plopped onto the couch. "Whew, I'm starved. Your turn to say the blessing."

"What happened? Are you telling me that he showed up this morning at the country club and apologized? Or no, there was a mix up. He didn't proposition you, did he? You jumped to conclusions like you always do and accused him of it. Right? When it wasn't true?"

"You're partly right. I was asked out to coffee, sure, but it wasn't by Mr. Upland. I thought it was, but you know me, like I can remember everyone I've ever met."

"We went to school with Mark *Upton.* Don't you remember?"

"I was busy in high school. How was I supposed to know everyone? Besides, I don't recognize a lot of people. I'm not good with faces."

"Or names."

"Or names." How could she argue with that? She wanted to keep things light and funny, that's the way she felt comfortable with everything. Anything serious or painful, well, that made her feel way too much. And once you started really feeling, then you had to face all the other emotions you were trying to avoid.

Avoidance was a very good policy. At least, she was doing fine avoiding the things that hurt the most. Take today. She didn't have to think about the fact that Brice Donovan might think she was a disaster, too, but he wanted to order a cake. She'd concentrate on the cake part, and try hard not to think about anything else.

Not that she was having the greatest luck with that.

"So what really happened?" Aubrey asked, taking possession of the remote before Ava could grab it and divert her with the movie. "It's okay. You can tell me. It isn't as bad as you think. Really."

Easy for Aubrey, who thought things through before she opened her mouth. Aubrey who never made a mistake of any kind, who never embarrassed herself, who never locked her keys in the car.

Remembering how Brice Donovan's voice had sounded, kind and not belittling, made the yuck of her morning fade a few shades.

"I'll tell you after the movie." Ava shrugged. Some things she didn't even want to talk about, even with her twin. That wasn't the way it was supposed to be, and she knew it made Aubrey sad to be shut out like that, but she didn't want to share every detail.

She wanted to do things right for a change—not just try really hard and then fail, but to really stay focused and careful and committed. One day, maybe she could be the girl who didn't make a mess, who didn't insult Bozeman's most eligible bachelor or who frustrated people so much they simply left her for good.

As Aubrey bowed her head, beginning the blessing, Ava bowed her head, too. But she added a silent prayer to Aubrey's. *Show me the way, Lord. Please, I don't want to mess up anymore. Show me how to be different. Better.*

There was no answer, just the click of the remote as Aubrey hit a button. The TV flared to life, showing a classic movie with a silver-screen hero. Maybe if she met a man like that, she might make an exception to her no-man policy.

She grabbed her fork and dug into the cashew chicken, but did she pay attention to the movie? No. Who was she thinking about?

Brice Donovan and how he'd looked like a real gentleman in his tux. How he'd looked like one of her forgotten dreams when he'd been standing in the full brightness of the morning sun, looking as vibrant and as substantial as a legend come true. But it was just a trick of the light. Legends didn't exist in real life, and real love didn't happen to her.

Chapter Four

It was a beautiful Monday morning, and Ava was on her way to meet the construction dudes. Okay, in truth, she was going to ply them with her special batch of homemade doughnuts and signature coffee. She might not be the brightest bulb in the pack, but she wasn't the dimmest. It was only common sense that people worked better when they were well fueled.

This renovation was a step toward her dream. Tangible and real, and all the hammering and sawing and dust to come would transform the dingy little place into a baker's delight. This was fabulous, something to celebrate, right?

Right. At least, she *should* be feeling so buoyant with happiness that she ought to be floating. But sadly her happiness felt subdued and superficial like icing on the cake, and nothing deeper. Why?

She'd been down a little ever since Brice Donovan's call. Did that make any sense?

No. So what was all this being sad stuff about? Concentrate on the positive, Ava.

She screeched into the closest parking space since her favorite spot—right beneath the shade of a broad-leafed maple—was already taken by a big forest-green pickup truck. It was the ostentatious kind that looked as if it cost more than a house. There was a lot of chrome glinting in the low-rising sun and big lights on top of a custom cab. It probably belonged to one of the construction guys.

Yep, there was one standing on the sidewalk with his back to her. He seemed to be looking over the front of the shop with a contractor's discerning eye.

She cut the engine and grabbed her cell from the console and her bag from the front passenger seat. It was still early, only ten minutes to seven. She'd have time to get the coffee canisters set up and the doughnuts laid out before the rest of the workers arrived. She elbowed the door open, stepped down from the seat and the second her shoe touched the ground she felt it. Something was wrong, but she couldn't put her finger on what.

The construction worker hadn't moved. He was still staring at the front windows—and she could see his reflection as clearly as she could see her own. He looked remarkably like Brice Donovan. That handsome face, sculpted cheekbones and chin, straight nose and strong jaw were all the same.

Except for one thing—how could that be Brice? It made no sense. She gave the door a shove to close it.

She had Brice Donovan on the brain. *That's* why her emotions were all off kilter. *That's* why she wasn't fully enjoying the beautiful morning or this first momentous day of construction.

Brice Donovan. It wasn't as if she even liked him a tiny bit. Really. So what was going on? Maybe it was stress, she decided as she circled around to the back of the vehicle and realized she hadn't hit the door release.

No problem. She looked down at her cell phone. Where were her keys?

The automatic locks clicked shut all on their own.

Great. Wonderful. Terrific. She'd done it again! Why wasn't she paying better attention?

Well, if she hadn't have been thinking of Brice Donovan then she wouldn't have been distracted. See? *This* is why she had to stick to her no-man policy—all the way. No exceptions. Even thinking of him just a little caused problems.

She leaned her forehead against the rear window and took a deep breath. All she needed was to call Aubrey. Plus, there was a silver lining in all this. At least this time she hadn't locked her cell phone in, too. Hey, it could be worse.

She flipped open her phone when a startling familiar baritone rumbled right behind her. "Let me guess. You're in need of rescuing again."

Brice Donovan? She turned around and there he was, looking totally macho in workmen's clothes. The lettering on the light gray T-shirt he wore said it all: D&M Construction, the name of the company she'd hired for the renovation. How on earth did he have a shirt with that company name? Did he work for them?

Then it hit her. Maybe the *D* stood for Donovan. *Wow.*

He jammed his hands into his pockets, emphasizing the muscled set of his shoulders. "You don't look happy to see me."

"Surprised." So surprised she had to lean against the fender for support. "What are you doing here?"

"Rafe Montgomery was going to do the job, but I sweet-talked him into trading."

"Lucky me." Ava's mind swirled. Montgomery must be the *M* in the company. Rafe had been a nice man who'd been her contact. "But why are you here in workman's clothes. Aren't you like an investment broker or something?"

"That would be my dad. Rafe Montgomery and I got to talking one night while we were studying for our graduate school exams. What we were really dreading wasn't taking the test, it was being cooped up in an office all day. Just like our dads. Don't get me wrong, I don't mind putting in a good hard day's work, but I felt put in a box. It wasn't for either of us. So we pooled our resources and went into business."

That was the most unlikely story she'd ever

heard. MBA dudes who built stuff? "I'd like to think you had woodworking training. A certificate of carpentry competence."

"I'm good at what I do, believe me."

Oh, she did believe him. And how was it possible that he looked even better dressed for work than he had the other day in a tux? Today he looked genuine, capable and very manly.

"Let me get a coat hanger." He strode to the green pickup and opened the crew-cab door. A big golden retriever tumbled out and ping-ponged in place in front of Brice, tongue lolling. "Whoa there, boy."

Okay, she melted. She couldn't help it—she was a softy when it came to dogs. "What's his name?"

Goofy brown eyes fastened on her. That big doggy mouth swung wide, showing dozens of sharp teeth. The huge canine launched toward her, tongue out and grinning, moving so fast he was a golden-brown blur.

"Rex, no! Come back here." Brice reached for his collar to catch him.

Too late.

Ava didn't have time to brace herself, because the dog was already leaping on her, plopping one front paw on either side of her neck, almost hugging her. His tongue swiped across her chin. Happy chocolate eyes studied hers with sheer joy.

"Brice, I'm in love with your dog." She couldn't help it. The big cuddly retriever hugged her harder before dropping down on all four paws. As if he knew how much he'd charmed her, he posed handsomely, staring up adoringly with those sweet eyes.

"Excuse him. He's very friendly. Too friendly." Brice grabbed his collar. "This may come as a shock to you but he failed every obedience class he's been in. From puppy school all the way up to the academy."

"Academy?"

"I hired professionals, but in the end, he won." Brice turned his attention to the retriever, his face softening, his big hand stroking over the crown of the canine's downy head. He received a few swipes of that lolling tongue and laughed. "Life's hard enough, isn't it? Without being told what to do every second of the day."

Ava couldn't believe it. The big, macho, most eligible bachelor was tough looking with all his masculine strength and charm, but she knew his secret. He was a big marshmallow underneath.

Not that she was interested. Really.

"This'll only take a second, now that I have the routine down." He took a wire hanger—she hadn't even noticed when he'd fetched it from his truck—and unbent it enough to slide it between the frame of the door and the roof.

True to his word, a few seconds later he'd hit the lock and was pulling her key from the ignition and silencing the alarm. He hit the back door release for her.

Okay, he was really a decent guy. On the surface anyway, and that's the only level on which she intended to know him. He was the *D* in D&M Construction, so that meant for better or worse, she was stuck with him. Not that she thought for a moment he actually did the hard work. No, he was probably more of a figurehead. He probably just oversaw projects. He was Roger Donovan's son, right?

She lifted the back and slid out the bakery box, and Rex bounded up to sniff at it.

"Hey, buddy, these are not for you." Ava might be charmed by the big cuddly dog, but she wasn't that big of a pushover. "Sit."

The retriever grinned up at her with every bit of charisma he possessed.

"Look at him drool. That can only mean one thing. There must be doughnuts in that box." There was Brice, as large as life, wrapping one big, powerful hand around the canine's blue nylon collar. "Need any help carrying those?"

"I suppose you like doughnuts, too."

"Guilty." His warm eyes and dazzling grin, those dimples and personality and his hard appearance made him look good down to the soul.

She had been fooled by this type of guy before, but not this time. "These are not for you. They are for your crew. For the men who actually work for a living instead of walking around owning companies."

"Hey, I work hard."

"I don't see a hammer." She reached for a second box, but he beat her to it. It was heavy with big thermos-type coffee canisters. "I see you eyeing the thermoses and no, you may not have any of that, either. Not unless you're a construction dude, and I don't see a tool belt strapped to your waist."

"That's not fair. My tools are in my truck."

She rolled her eyes. "Oh, *sure* they are."

Brice shut the door and hit the remote. Rex bounced at his hip, the dog's gaze glued to the pink bakery box. "You know I'm the on-site manager of this project, right?"

"I'll have to see it to believe it." She snapped ahead of him with that quick-paced walk of hers, her yellow sneakers squeaking with each step. "I still don't get why you're here. Why I'm plagued with you and that dog of yours."

She eyed him like a judge awaiting a guilty verdict, but she didn't fool him. Not one bit. He saw in her eyes and in the hint of her smile what she was trying to hide. He wasn't the only one wondering.

Maybe he wasn't the only one wishing.

"Where do you want these?" he asked of the stuff he carrying.

She gestured to the worn wooden counter in front of them, where she'd set the bakery box and was lifting the lid.

He did as she asked and nearly went weak in the knees at the aroma wafting out from the open box. Sweet cake doughnuts, the comforting bite of chocolate, the richness of custard and the mouth-watering sweet huckleberries that glistened like fat blue jellybeans.

"Where did you get these?" The question wasn't past his lips before he knew the answer. "You made these. You."

"Okay, that's so surprising? I'm a baker. Hel-*lo*." She rolled her eyes at him, but it was cute, the way she shook her head as if she simply didn't know about him. Yep, he knew what she was trying to do. Because whatever was happening between them felt a little scary, like standing on the edge of a crumbling precipice and knowing while the fall was certain, the how and what of the landing was not.

She pulled a bag of paper plates from her big shoulder bag, ripped it open and pulled out a plate. She slid the berries-and-cream-topped doughnut onto the plate and handed it to him. "I saw you eyeing it."

Had she noticed how he'd been looking at her? He thought she was two hundred times sweeter than that doughnut. "How about some cups?"

"Here." She pulled a bag of them from her mammoth bag. "Which doughnut should I give your dog?"

Rex gave a small bark of delight and sat on his haunches like the best dog in the world. His doggy gaze was glued on the bottom corner of the bakery box.

"He'd take every last one. Don't trust him if you leave that box uncovered."

"Oh, he's a good guy. It's you I don't trust," she

said with a hint of a grin. "You said you traded with Mr. Montgomery. I want to know why."

Just his luck. He filled two cups with sweetened, aromatic coffee and handed her one. "How about grace, first?"

"I've already had my breakfast." She took the coffee.

Their fingertips brushed and it was a little like being hit by a lightning strike from a blue sky. His heartbeat lurched to a stop. What was it about Ava that seemed to make his world stand still?

She gave him another judgmental look like a prim schoolmarm as she put a glazed doughnut on a second plate. Rex's tail thumped like a jackhammer against the scarred tile floor. She knelt to set the plate on the floor.

"What a nice polite gentleman," she praised, and gave him a pat.

Rex sat a moment to further fool Ava into thinking he was a perfect dog before he wolfed down the doughnut in two bites.

"You're welcome," she said as she patted him again and removed the plate. "Oh, some of the men are driving up now. Good."

Brice tried not to let it bother him that she disregarded him completely as she disappeared through the kitchen door. This was *not* how most single ladies reacted to him. He considered the steaming cup of coffee he held and the plate with the delectable doughnut.

Lord, I'm gonna need help with this one. If it's Your will, please show me the way.

The doors swung closed as if in answer, swinging open again to show a glimpse of Ava, washed in sunlight from the large window. Inexplicably, the sun shone brighter.

Could the morning be going any more perfectly? The homemade doughnuts were a hit. With promises of more sweet surprises for tomorrow morning, Ava made sure the fridge was stocked with plenty of liquids—it was important to keep the workers hydrated—and gathered up her stuff.

Time to get out of their way. Dust was already flying. Walls were already missing. As curious as she was to see absolutely everything, she knew she'd only be in the way. Besides, she had to work at her family's bookstore because she had her share of the rent and utilities to pay at month's end. Not to mention her car payment. Oh, and credit card payments. And her school loans. She grabbed her bag and was in the middle of hunting down her keys when she suddenly realized she wasn't alone.

"Ava, I'm glad I caught you." There was Brice, shouldering through the door. "Before you go, I want to go over your final plans."

"I already did that with Mr. Montgomery. When we talked the other day on the phone, you know, after Chloe's wedding, you said you wanted to stop by on

Monday morning. I assumed that meant you were interested in ordering a cake. But this is why, isn't it?"

"I can order a cake if you want."

"It isn't what I want that's the question." Really, that grin of his was infectious. Dashing and charming and utterly disarming. What was a girl to do? How was she supposed to *not* smile back? She was helpless here. *Lord, give me strength, please.* "I haven't forgotten that you tried to ask me out. I mean, I know you changed your mind once I started insulting you."

"The post traumatic stress is better, by the way. Although standing in this kitchen might give me a flashback or two." His grin deepened right along with his dimples. "You're questioning why I'm here, right? Remember I said that you made my sister happy with her wedding cake?"

"I do." Leery, that's what she had to be. On guard. The kindness of his smile was like a tractor beam pulling her in. If she wasn't careful, she was going to start liking this man.

Liking men at all—even platonically—wasn't a part of her no-man policy. Because that's how it had happened with Ken, the chef she dated about five months back, and that had ended in disaster. If she didn't learn lessons from her ten billion mistakes, how was she ever going to feel better about herself?

Brice came closer, his dog trailing after him. "You made Chloe happy, and now I want to return the favor."

Okay, she could buy that reason. It was actually a nice reason. Which only made him a nicer man in her eyes.

He set a coffee cup down on the metal table between them and gave it a shove in her direction, obviously meant for her. She hadn't noticed what he'd been carrying.

How could she have not noticed that he was hauling with him a rolled up blueprint, too?

Keep your mind on business, Ava, she ordered herself. Really, it was that smile of Brice's. It ought to come with a surgeon general's warning. Beware: Might Have The Gravitational Pull Of A Black Hole And Suck You Right In.

"I know you've gone over the plans with my partner." Brice plopped the blueprints on the metal work table and spread out them out with quick efficiency. He anchored each corner with a battered tape measure and hammer he plucked from his tool belt. "But what I want to know is the dream of what you want. The heart of it. Beyond the computer-generated drawings of this place."

Okay, that wasn't what she expected and it disarmed her even more. Emotions tangled in her throat and made her voice thick and strange sounding. "I showed Mr. Montgomery a few pictures of what I had in mind."

"I'd like to see them."

Their gazes met, and a connection zinged between them. A sad ache rolled through her and she didn't know why. She refused to let herself ask. Instead, she fumbled through the top drawer in the battered cabinets. She'd left the magazine pictures here to show the woodworker, just in case.

But turning her back to him gave her no sense of privacy or relief from the aching she felt. Somehow she managed to face him again, but her hands were shaking. She didn't want to think too hard on the reason for that, either. "Here. I'm not looking for exactly this. But something warm and whimsical and unique. In my price range."

She spread the three full-color pictures on the metal table, turning them so they were right side up for his inspection. Long ago, she'd torn them from magazines she'd come across, tucking them away for the when and if of this dream. The white frame of the pages had dulled to yellow over time, and the ragged edges where she'd torn them from the magazine looked tattered. But the bright glass displays and the intricate woodwork remained as bright and as promising as ever.

"It's probably beyond my budget, I know, that's what Mr. Montgomery said. But he thought he could scale it down and still get some of the feeling of the craftsmanship."

Brice said nothing as he studied the photos, sipping his coffee, taking his time. "Why baking? Why not open a bistro? Or stay working at your family's bookstore?"

Surprise shot across her face. "You know about

the bookstore? Wait, Chloe knows. She probably told you."

That wasn't exactly true. Everyone knew about the bookstore. Ava's grandmother's family, a wealthy and respected family and one of the area's original settlers, had owned the store forever. "I need to know what this means to you before I start on the woodwork. Isn't that what you do before you design a cake for someone?"

"Exactly." She took a sip of the sweetened coffee and studied him through narrowed eyes, as if she were truly seeing him for the first time.

He could see her heart, shining in her eyes, whole and dazzling. He leaned closer. Couldn't stop himself.

She turned one of the pictures around to study. "You wouldn't understand what I want, being Bozeman's most eligible bachelor and all."

"You know, I have relatives who work on the local paper. That's where the list came from. I had nothing to do with it. I'm just a working man, so I bet I can understand. Try me."

A cute little furrow dug in between her eyes, over the bridge of her nose. Adorable, she shrugged one slim shoulder, and for a moment she looked lost. *Sad.* "My mom really wasn't happy being a wife and mother. I know that. But when I was little it felt like I was the one who made her unhappy. I was always spilling stuff and knocking into furniture and forgetting things. Not that I've changed that much." She shrugged again. "This isn't what you want to hear."

"This is exactly right. Exactly what I want to know."

He laid his hand over hers, feeling the warm silk of her skin and the cool smoothness of the magazine page. One picture was of bistro tables washed in sunlight, framed by golden, scrolled wood and crisp white clouds of curtains. It looked like something out of a children's story book, where evil was easily defeated, where every child was loved and where love always won.

That's what he knew she saw on the page, he knew because he could see her heart so clearly.

She drew in a ragged breath, her voice thin with emotion, her eyes turning an arresting shade of indigo. "One thing that always went right was when I was with Mom in the kitchen. She wasn't much of a baker, but I had spent a lot of time with Gran in the kitchen, she taught me to bake, and I liked the quiet time. Measuring sugar and sifting flour. Getting everything just right."

She paused as if noticing for the first time that his hand still covered hers. She didn't try to move away. Did she know how vulnerable she looked? How good and true? He didn't think so. He feared his heart, hurting so much for her, would never be the same.

"This reminds you of baking with your Mom," he said.

"Sort of. I remember the kitchen smelled wonderful when the cookies or the cakes were cooling. And afterwards there was the frosting to whip up and the decorating to do. It's the one thing I could always do right. It made everyone happy, for how ever little time that happiness lasted, it was there."

"And then your mother left?"

Ava gently tugged her hand out from beneath his. She lowered her gaze, veiled her heart. That was a scandal of huge proportion. Everybody had known at the time, and in a small city that was really just one big small town, everybody still remembered although twenty years had passed. "I want this to be like a place where customers feel like they've stepped into a storybook. Not childish, just—" She couldn't think of the word.

"You want a place where it feels as if wishes can come true."

How did he know that? Ava took a shaky breath and tucked away the honesty she shouldn't have hauled out like dirty laundry in a basket. She was *so* not a wishing kind of girl. Not anymore.

She grabbed her bag again, not remembering when exactly it had slipped from her shoulder to the floor. "I'd better get going. I'm late for my shift at the bookstore."

"Do I make you uncomfortable?"

"Yes." The word popped out before she could stop it.

He winced. "Well, that's not my intention. We got off on the wrong foot. Is that's what's bothering you?"

"No. Yes."

"Which is it?"

"I don't know." All she knew was that he felt *way* too close, although she'd crossed half of the kitchen on the way to the door and it still didn't make any difference. She took a shaky breath. "I should have recognized you. I mean, I'm usually so busy in my own little world, I don't notice everything I should."

"Well, I didn't introduce myself, so when you think about it, it could be all my fault."

"You're being too nice."

"That's better than being Mr. Yuck, right?"

"Maybe."

That made his dimples flash. "What do you do with your time, besides baking incredible cakes?"

"Hang out with my sisters, mostly. Doing my part to contribute to consumer debt. That kind of thing." And that was all she was going to share with him because anything else would be way too personal. "Okay, what did I do with my keys?"

"I might have 'em." He reached into his back pocket and then there they were in the palm of his hand.

Oops. It looked like she would have to move closer to him to get them. Her chest tightened and her emotions felt like one big aching mess. Was it because of the story she'd told him, about baking with her mother? Or was he the reason?

She knew the answer simply by looking at him. His appearance—the worn T-shirt, battered Levi's and beat-up black workboots—all shouted tough guy, but in a really good, hard-working way. Add that to his kindness and class—and he was totally wishable.

Not that she was wishing.

As he strode toward her with the slow measured gait of a hunter, she didn't feel stalked. No, she felt *drawn*. As if he'd gathered up her tangled heartstrings and gave them a gentle shake. There were no more knots, just one simple, honest feeling running up those strings and straight into her heart.

She didn't want to be drawn to any man. Especially not him.

She grabbed the keys, careful to scoop them from his hand without any physical contact. But something had changed between them and she couldn't deny it.

"Thanks," she said in a practically normal-sounding voice. "You have my cell number if there's a problem, right?"

"Right."

She could feel him watching her as she yanked open the door. Rex bounded toward her and she almost forgot about Brice. She knelt down to give his head a good rubbing. "It was very nice meeting you, boy. I'll bring some muffins tomorrow. Is that all right by you?"

Rex lapped her cheek and panted in perfect agreement.

She had one foot over the threshold when Brice's voice called her back. "See you tomorrow, Ava. And thanks for sharing a cup of coffee with me."

Coffee. That made her screech to a total halt. Her mind sat there, idling. Isn't that what he'd wanted to do in the beginning? He'd wanted to get to know her over a cup of coffee.

And he had.

She wanted to leap to the quick conclusion that she'd been tricked. But it wasn't that simple. She'd been the one to bring the coffee in the first place. It was her coffee, her kitchen, her renovation project. It was her heart she had to hold onto as she took the other step through the door and closed Brice Donovan from her sight.

Chapter Five

Ava burst through the employee's entrance door in the back of the Corner Christian Bookstore. The big problem? Her oldest sister was heating a cup of tea in the break room's microwave and she had *that* look. The one where she frowned, shook her head slowly from side to side as if this was exactly what she expected.

"Oops, I'm late." Ava slid the bakery box onto the small battered Formica table. "My bad. But I brought chocolate."

"That doesn't begin to make up for it." The corner of Katherine's mouth twitched, as if she were holding back a smile. "What am I going to do with you?"

"Nothing. I'm your little sister and you love me."

"Not at much as Aubrey," she teased. "Aubrey showed up twenty-three minutes early for her shift."

"True." Aubrey appeared from the other doorway that led to the floor. "I smell doughnuts. The doughnuts that were missing from our kitchen this morning. I came back from the stables and had nothing to eat. You didn't have to take every last one with you."

"Hey, the real question is why would you walk by a kitchen full of boxed doughnuts and not take any in the first place?" With a wink, Ava shoved open the small employee's closet and dumped her bag on the floor.

"What could have possessed me, I wonder?" Aubrey flipped open the box and stole a chocolate huckleberry custard. "The construction dudes were—"

"Cool. Loved the doughnuts. Started beating down walls with their sledgehammer thingies right away." Ava grabbed a cup from the upper cabinet and filled it from the sink tap.

Don't think of Brice, she ordered herself. Too late. There he was in her mind's eye. Standing in her kitchen, looking like a good man, radiating character. Normally, she'd be *so* interested, but if she let herself like him, that would be just another huge mistake in a long, endless string of disasters.

Don't start wishing now, she told herself, letting her big sister Katherine take the mug from her hands and slip it into the microwave to heat.

"You look down," Katherine commented as she added honey to her steaming teacup, her engagement ring sparkling. "That can't be good. This is your first day of renovation. You should be excited. What's going on?"

"Uh-oh." Aubrey had a twin moment.

Great. Somehow she had telebeamed her thoughts to her twin; they seemed to share brain cells. Ava felt the humiliation creeping through her all over again. "Don't say it. Let's just not go into it."

Ava could sense Katherine's question hovering in the air unspoken between them, wanting to know what was wrong and how she could help. Dear Katherine meant well, wanting to take care of everyone and fixing what she could, but what do you do when you know there's no solution to a problem?

You refocus yourself, that's what, and concentrate on preventing disasters. There was Brice Donovan again, flashing across her brain pan. Definitely disaster material.

Hayden, Katherine's soon-to-be stepdaughter, poked her head around the door. "Hey, like, Spence is totally freaking out. There's no one out there to ring up and stuff."

"So? Our brother is always freaking out."

"I'll go," Aubrey said. "I'm supposed to be watching the front anyway. I'll take this with me, though." With a grin she slipped past the teenager with her chocolate-covered doughnut in hand.

"Like that's going to make Spence happy." The kid shrugged her gangly shoulders. "Maple bars, too? Cool, Ava."

"I knew they were your favorite, not that I like

you or anything." Ava hid her smile, knowing she wasn't so successful.

Hayden grinned, snatched a doughnut. "Thanks!" she called over her shoulder as she disappeared back into the stacks.

Talk about weird. "Are you ready to be a stepmom?" Ava already knew the answer, but it was called a diversionary tactic. She *so* did not want to talk about her shop, her dreams, and how it had all gotten tangled up with Mr. Wishable. "You'll be marrying Jack in two more months."

"I know. Time is melting way and it feels as if I'm never going to have everything ready for the wedding." Katherine waited for the microwave to ding. She opened the door, dropped a tea bag into the steaming water and left it on the counter to steep. "But I'm more than ready to be a stepmom. Hayden is a part of Jack. How could I not love her? Speaking of which, how are the designs for my cake coming along?"

Okay, another topic to avoid. "I'm working on it. Honest."

"I have all the faith in the world in you, sweetie."

Wasn't that the problem? "I've got some great sketches, but I've got a few more ideas I want to work out before we sit back down."

"Do you know what we should do?" Katherine pushed the plastic bear-shaped bottle of honey along the counter. "We'll all go out to a nice dinner, my treat. To celebrate."

"Celebrate what?"

Katherine shook her head, as if she couldn't believe it. "The first day of construction on your shop? This has been your dream forever, right?"

"I can't tonight. I have a consultation. Maybe later, though? Besides, you're just in a good mood because you've found Mr. Dream Come True. Not everyone is as lucky." She didn't mean to sound wistful, really. She was deeply happy for her sister. Katherine deserved a good man and a happy marriage. And, seeing that it had happened for her sister after all this time, it *almost* gave a girl a little hope it could happen to her.

Not that she'd go around praying for it, because she'd tried that route before. She had a gift for prayer. She might make a mess of everything she touched, she might show up late for work and forget where she put her keys, but what she prayed for almost always happened. Hence her last relationship disasters with Mike, Brett and Ken. Before that, Isaiah, Christian and Lloyd. It was that old adage, be careful what you wish for. Which was why she wasn't, not even silently, wishing. Really.

"I know something isn't right." Katherine frowned as if she were trying to figure out what. "I know you've got to be under a lot of pressure getting your business off the ground, but you know you're not alone, right? You say the word and we're right with you. In fact, you might not have a chance to say the word before we barge in."

Was she blessed with her awesome family or what? Ava's eyes burned. She was grateful to the Lord for her wonderful sisters. "You know me. I know how to holler."

"Excellent." Katherine brushed some of Ava's windblown hair out of her eyes. "Whatever's got you down, remember you are just the way God made you. And that makes you perfectly lovable, sweetie. Trust me."

She didn't know about being perfectly lovable but she did know that her sister—her family—was on her perfectly lovable list. Blessings she gave thanks for every day of her life. Katherine's words meant everything.

The morning had been perfect. The construction workers were hard-working family men who were very happy with the box of doughnuts. And— surprise!—Brice looked like a good boss and a hard worker himself. She was confident that the renovation would be terrific when it was done.

She was the problem since she wavered on what she said she wanted. No, she wasn't exactly wavering. But she'd *almost* given in to wishing and that was just as bad. She had to be more careful. More determined.

A deep, frustrated huff sounded at the inner door. It was Spence, glowering. "There you two are. Ava, you're late. For, what, the fifteenth shift in a row?"

"Probably. Sorry." Ava couldn't argue. She upended the plastic bear over her cup and gave it a hard squeeze. "But I'm here now, so that's good, right? I mean, it could be worse. I could be even later."

That was the logic that always confounded Spence. His Heathcliff personality couldn't seem to understand and he stormed away.

She wasn't fooled. His bark was much worse than his bite.

"He's under a lot of pressure," Katherine excused him as she grabbed a cinnamon twist from the box on her way to the front. "Thanks for the goodies, cutie."

Alone in the break room, Ava took a sip of her tea, but the chamomile blend didn't soothe her. She dumped in more honey, and that didn't do the trick either. A big piece of sadness sat square in the middle of her chest, stronger after having been with Brice.

His words came back to her now. *You want a place where it feels as if wishes could come true.* He'd said what was in her heart.

How had he known?

At a loss, she headed out front. She had bills to pay and dreams to dream—and a no-man policy to stick to.

Ava had lingered in his thoughts all through the work day, all of Brice's waking hours and into the next morning. He hadn't looked forward to strapping on his tool belt this much in a long time. Though he liked his work, it was the prospect of seeing Ava that made the difference.

His commitment to this renovation project was

about more than work. He wanted to do a good job with it—hands down, customer satisfaction was job one. But beyond that, he wanted to do his best to give Ava her dream. Listening to her talk about baking with her mom—the mom who had run off to Hollywood with the youngest daughter decades ago and had never been heard from since—was like a sign from above pointing the way to win her heart.

He wondered if Ava had any idea how purely her inner beauty shone when she talked about being happy like that? In wanting again, for others and for herself, a joy-filled place where wishes could come true?

She was a different kind of woman than he was used to. Whitney had been exactly what his mom had wanted for him. She was from a respectable family, from money older than the state of Montana. The right schools and the proper social obligations and charity work. But in the end, she'd been wrong for him. Wrong for the man he really was, not Roger Donovan's son, but a Montanan born and raised, who liked his life a little more comfortable and far less showy.

The shop had a decimated look to it, even gilded by the golden peach of the newly rising sun. The interior walls were bare down to the studs, which glowed like honey in the morning light. The white dip and rise of electrical wire ran like a clothesline the length of the room. Dust coated the windows, but he could see the promise. See her dream.

Rex romped to the front door, springing in place with excitement. His tongue rolled out of his mouth as he panted, and since Brice was taking too long, pawed at the door handle.

"Hold on there, bud. I'm eager to see Ava, too."

The retriever gave a low bark when he heard Ava's name.

Yeah, at least the dog liking her won't be an issue the way it was with Whitney. Yet another sign, Brice figured as he picked through his mammoth ring of work keys, found the one for the shop and unlocked the door. Whitney hadn't been fond of big, bouncing, sometimes slobbery dogs. Brice was.

The second the door was open an inch, Rex hit it at a dead run and launched through the open kitchen doors. There on the work table was a bright pink bakery box. That explained the retriever's eagerness. They may have missed Ava, but she'd left a consolation prize.

She'd come before his shift started, left her baking and skedaddled. Apparently, there was a good reason. Like maybe the comment he'd made about finally getting to talk with her over coffee. Maybe— just maybe—he shouldn't have pointed that out.

Right when he'd thought he was making progress with her, getting to know her, letting her know the kind of man he was, he'd hit a brick wall.

Apparently Ava wasn't as taken with him as he was with her.

Wow. That felt like a hard blow to his sternum.

Here was the question: Did he pursue this or not? Sure, they'd gotten off on the wrong foot when she'd mistaken him for Chloe's groom, but even after that, she'd been determined to put some distance between them.

Face it, this was one-sided. He'd stood right here in this kitchen and got to know her, seen right through to her dreams. He was captivated by her. He was falling in serious like with her.

But now? She was missing in action.

Rex's bark echoed in the vacant kitchen.

"Okay, okay." Brice popped open the huge bakery box. "Only one, and I mean it this time. All this baked stuff can't be good for you—"

He fell silent at the treats inside the box. She'd promised muffins, but these weren't like anything he'd ever seen. They were huge muffins shaped like cute, round monsters. They had ropy icing for hair, big goofy eyes, a potato nose and a wide grin. Two dozen monster faces stared up at him, colorful and whimsical.

Ava made the ordinary unusual and fun. He liked that about her. Very much.

He'd been praying, to find a good woman to love and marry. Have a few kids. Live a happy life. That had been part of his plan for a long time, but it just hadn't worked out for one reason or another. In fact, it hadn't worked out for such a length of time that began to feel as if his prayer was destined to remain unanswered.

The front door swung open and heavy boots pounded against the floor, echoing in the demolished room. It was Tim, the electrician. "Hey, where are those muffins she promised?"

"In here."

"I gotta tell ya," Tim said as he dropped his tool bags on the floor, "this might be the best job we've done yet. The doughnuts yesterday were something. You think she's gonna keep bakin' for us?" Tim's jaw dropped in disbelief when he saw the muffins. "Look at that. Think anyone would mind if I took one home for my little girl? She'd get a kick out of that."

Brice realized that Ava had made five times the number of muffins they needed for their small work crew. "Go for it."

"Cool." Tim grabbed a mammoth monster muffin and took a bite. "Mmm," he said around a full mouth, as if surprised by how good it tasted.

Not that Brice was surprised by that. He flipped open his phone and dialed. While he waited for the call to connect, he took a muffin for Rex on the way out the back door. The sunshine felt hot and dry as he sat on the back step and unwrapped the muffin. The dog gobbled his muffin in three bites.

Ava picked up on the sixth ring. "Hi there. Is there a problem at the shop?"

Caller ID, he guessed. "A problem? You could say that."

"What's wrong? I was there and everything

looked fine. Okay, it was like a total wreck, but it's supposed to look like that, right?"

"Right. That wasn't the kind of problem I meant." He leaned back, resting his spine against the building. He wondered where she was. A lot of clanging sounded in the background. "You left a box of monsters behind. Why didn't you stay and say hello?"

"I didn't want to be in the way."

"I hope you didn't feel uncomfortable with me yesterday. You know I like you."

"I'm trying to ignore that."

"Is there any particular reason for that?"

"Well, you're doing the renovation on my shop, for starters."

"Good reason. Look, I don't want you to feel uncomfortable. Not around me. Not around my men. Not when it comes to the work we're doing for you."

"Sure, I know that."

It didn't seem as if she did. She sounded as vulnerable as she'd looked yesterday when she'd been talking about her baking. Okay, so maybe what he felt wasn't a two-way street. "How about you and I agree to be friends. Would that make you more comfortable?"

"Friends? Uh, sure. Wait." He could imagine her biting her bottom lip while she thought, the cute little furrow digging in between her eyes. "You mean like platonic friends."

"I mean that whatever this is going on between us, let's put in on hold until your renovation is done. That way you don't have to come to your own shop before 6:45 a.m. just to avoid me."

"I wasn't necessarily avoiding *you*." Ava knew her voice sounded thin and honest. She was no good at subterfuge of any kind. Another reason she'd never understood men who had hidden agendas. "You see, it's not you. It's me. All me."

"You want to explain that?" he asked in that kind way he had, but he obviously didn't understand.

There it was, doom, hovering right in front of her, and its name was Brice Donovan.

"It's just that—" she blurted out, nearly losing hold of her grocery cart in the dairy aisle. "I have the worst luck dating. If there's a loser anywhere near me, he'll be the one I think is nice. I'm like a disaster magnet. That's why I have a policy."

"What policy? I don't understand."

She felt her heart weakening. She liked this man—and wasn't that the exact problem? She had to be totally tough. Cool. Focused. Strong. That's what she had to be. Strong enough to stick to her guns. "It's an iron-clad, non-negotiable no-man, no-dating policy."

"That's a pretty strict policy. There's a good reason for it, huh?"

Her throat tightened. When she spoke, she knew she sounded as if she were struggling. "Yeah. Nothing horrible, just disappointing. I don't want to spend my life believing in a man's goodness and being blind to any terrible faults that I just can't see until it's too late. You see, it's like being color-blind. I'm just…" She didn't know what to say.

Apparently Brice didn't either. No sound came from his end of the connection. Nothing at all.

"I'm sorry." That came out strangled sounding.

So she was never going to be a tough business woman. She wasn't a tough anything. Sadness hit her like the cold from the refrigerated dairy case. Was she disappointed?

Surprisingly, yes.

"Okay, then. I'll call you if we have any questions over here." He broke the silence, sounding business as usual, but beneath, she thought she heard disappointment, too.

Maybe it was best not to think about that, she thought as she closed her phone, dumped it into her bag and put the milk jug into her cart. She couldn't say why she would be feeling deflated, because she did the right thing by putting him off. She just had to stay focused on her goals and her path in life, she thought as she grabbed a carton of whipping cream.

Her phone rang again and she went fishing for it in her messy tote. Luckily it was still ringing when she found it. She didn't recognize the number on the screen. "Hello?"

"Uh, yes," came a refined woman's voice. "My name is Maxime Frost and I was at Chloe Donovan's wedding. Brice highly recommended you, and I just *had* to call. We simply must have one of your cakes for my Carly's wedding."

"I'm sure I can design something both you and Carly will love."

She wrote down an appointment time on the inside of her checkbook and ended the call. How about that? Brice had recommended her in spite of the mistaken identity incident.

Just when she thought she was sure she'd made the right decision to stick to her no-date policy, look what happened. He made her start wishing all over again—and reconsidering.

Chapter Six

Everyone was at the restaurant by the time she got there, seated in a big table at the back, between a cozy intersection of booths. Of course, she was late because she was time-challenged. From the head of the table, Spence spotted her first and his dour frown darkened a notch. He highly prized timeliness. Katherine sat between him and her fiancé, Jack Munroe. Seated next to her dad, the teenaged Hayden gave a finger wave.

Ava lifted her hand to finger wave back but the sight of the appetizers in platters placed in three parts of the table stopped her in her tracks. "I can't believe you ordered without me."

"You're twenty minutes late." Spence huffed. "The assistant manager wasn't going to hold the reservation just for you."

Personally, this was why she thought Spence

wasn't married, but now was probably not the time to mention it. "Oops. Sorry." She didn't bother to explain the extra appointment she squeezed in, and that she'd left a message on Aubrey's phone that she'd be late, and there had been a major traffic snarl from some wild moose who was wandering Glenrose Street. It was easier to endure Spence's scowl.

She dropped into the empty seat next to her twin. "Do you check your messages?"

"I was out at the studio and lost track of time. I barely got here myself." Aubrey grabbed the platter in front of her and began sliding a stack of deep-fried zucchini slices onto Ava's plate. "Don't worry about Spence. It's that assistant manager who works here. The one that had that date with Katherine long ago and it didn't go well? He's always snippy with us. The construction—"

"Is going well." Ava paused to bow her head and gave a quick grace, since she'd missed Spence's blessing.

Aubrey spooned a heap of creamy dip next to the zucchini slices on Ava's plate. "And how's Brice?"

"Fine, I guess. I didn't see him today."

"And that wouldn't be because you're avoiding him?"

"I'm not avoiding him." It wasn't true but she wanted it to be. "Fine, I just avoided him for the day. Maybe I'll try again tomorrow."

"He's supposed to be this great guy. Wasn't he this year's most eligible bachelor or something?"

"Let's not talk about him." She glanced around the table to see if everyone was straining to listen. They were. "Later, okay?"

Katherine spoke up. "Didn't you do a wedding cake for Brice's sister?"

"Yeah. Just." Like she wanted to talk about it? *This* was the downside of being in a big family. Nothing was secret for long. "He's the contractor doing the renovation."

Spence leaned in. "You mean it's his *company* doing the renovation. He's not doing the actual work. He's an owner."

"No, he's like the on-site manager guy. Trust me, he had a hammer and everything." She hedged because everyone in her family but Aubrey was *way* too eager to marry her off. "Chloe recommended the company."

It didn't look like anyone at the table was fooled by that.

Katherine passed her hunky fiancé a platter of mozzarella sticks. "I thought Brice Donovan was engaged."

"No," Aubrey dragged a zucchini slice through a puddle of dip. "I read in the paper over a year ago that she called it off. The wedding was cancelled something like two days before it was supposed to happen. That had to be very hard for both of them."

Ava couldn't seem to swallow. The part of her that was afraid of getting close to him wanted to use this new piece of news as a reason to keep away from him. He'd already had one failed relationship. He was probably at fault, and she didn't need some flawed guy, right? On the surface, it sounded like the best reasoning.

But she knew it wasn't. Brice was a good guy— that much was clear. The real question was, how far down did that kindness go? Was it superficial, or the real thing?

The cracked pieces of her heart ached with a wish she couldn't let herself voice. Brice had a lot of redeeming qualities, so what? She had to resist. What she had to do was clear every thought of him from her mind. His every image from her memory. No more thoughts of Brice Donovan allowed.

"Good evening, McKaslin family," said a familiar voice behind her. Brice's voice.

Of course.

Why did it have to be him? She felt as if she'd been hit with the debris from a fast approaching tornado. She couldn't outrun it, escape it and there was no hope of avoiding it as Brice Donovan stepped into sight.

To her surprise her brother stood, nodding a greeting. "Good to see you again, Brice. Would you care to join us, or are you here with your family?"

"With family. It's my mother's birthday, but thanks for the invite. I just spotted Ava and I thought I'd come over. Let her know a few things about the job today, if she's got time before her meal arrives."

Ava could feel the power of his presence, stronger than the earth's gravity holding her feet to the floor. "Do I have time?" she asked her twin.

"I ordered for you," Aubrey explained. "Take your phone and you two go talk. I'll call you when the meal arrives."

Okay, it sounded like a good plan, but there was a downside here—did she want to be alone with Brice? No. Was she mentally prepared to be alone with him? Not a chance.

She grabbed her plate and her phone and followed him to the more casual patio area, where there were plenty of tables available. Brice nodded toward one of the waiters, who gestured to a set of unoccupied tables along the railing.

"I was hoping to catch you tomorrow morning." Brice was entirely too close as he leaned to pull out a chair for her. "But seeing you charge through the restaurant a few minutes ago seemed like a sign. I hope you don't mind the intrusion."

"Nope." What she minded was being alone with him. How was she going to hold onto her policy now? She caught a hint of his spicy aftershave. "After all, we've agreed to be friends."

"Exactly." He smiled his killer smile, the one with the dimples.

Did he know what that did to a woman? It made every innocent, friendly thought vanish and the ones about sweet romance and marriage proposals surge forth like a hurricane hitting shore. That part of her, which always panicked when she got too close to anyone new, started to tremble.

There was no need to panic. This was only business, right? Except as he helped her scootch her chair up to the table, it definitely didn't feel friendly.

He took the chair across the table from her, and a girl might think that would be safer, with the span of the table between them, but somehow he seemed closer. Much too close.

Don't wish, she reminded herself and bit into a zucchini slice. "If it's bad news about the renovation, you can't just spring it on me. It's best to work up to it. Want some?"

"Sure." He grabbed a coated, deep-fried slice and crunched into it. "I have some suggestions for changes for the finished woodwork. What Rafe drew up for you is nice, but it's plain."

"It's what I can afford."

"You can afford this, too." He took another slice. His manner was casual, his overall tone was friendly, but there was something intense beneath the surface, something that hadn't been there before. "I think you'll be happier with it. It won't add any time if I get started now. I mostly do the jobs with custom woodwork."

"I'm still trying to picture that. I know, I've seen you with a tool belt, but it doesn't still compute." She said this without thinking and watched his face harden. Not in a mean way, but guarded, like she'd struck a sore spot. "Don't get me wrong. There's a lot of integrity working to perfect a craft and doing your best. It's how I justify my baking. But I look at you and think, white-collar professional."

"It's a big issue in my family right now. My mom and dad have always just assumed I'd step into place at the family business and take over the firm when Dad's ready to retire. And he's starting to think about it, so they're starting to get serious."

"Aren't they supportive of what you're doing now?"

"They're tolerating it."

"I can't imagine that." Ava dragged a zucchini slice through the dip and bit into it. "My family is everything to me. I would be nothing without them."

"You seem tight with your sisters."

"Yeah. I'd never be able to open my own bakery without my family's help. I got my business loan from my grandmother—talk about fear of failure. I don't want to let her down. And Spence helped me with my business plan and buying the property. My sisters are helping me with the finishing stuff. Katherine took me to all the flea markets and swap meets and secondhand stores in the state, I think, and we got a bunch of bistro tables and chairs that Aubrey is refinishing for me in her studio. My step-sister Danielle has promised to make the window blinds and valences. That kind of thing. And that's not including the pep talks when I need them."

"So, they've got a lot of confidence in you. It

must be nice to have the people you love most wanting what will make you happy."

"It is." Ava's eyes shone with emotion and she dunked her zucchini into the dip. "It's also a lot of people to disappoint. Something I could never stand to do."

He could see that about her. Brice's throat tightened. "I can't stand how much this has upset my parents either. It's been a huge strain on our relationship."

"They want the best for you, though?"

He could see from the hopeful trust in her eyes that she didn't understand. "They do. I know they love me, but the truth is, I'm not what they hoped for in a son. I wrestled with it for a long time. I tried things their way, but I'm not cut out for spending a day in an office, investing other people's money. I like the work I do, but they see it as too blue collar."

"And that would be wrong because…?"

He swallowed his embarrassment over his parents. They were too set in their ways and opinions to change. He tried to dismiss the pain behind it, and the weight of his father's disappointments. His father who was a good, loving dad. Love and family were always complicated. "Dad thinks I'm not going to be happy unless I have a white-collar career, but I think it's the appearance thing. They care too much what other people think."

"It's hard to know other people think you're a

dope or a loser. It has happened to me too many times to count. I've become sort of numb to it."

He choked down a hoot of laughter. She said it with a twinkle in her eyes. She always surprised him. "Exactly. I've become a little numb on this subject, where my parents are concerned. My mom is still holding out hope I'll come to my senses and go to law school or medical school. Or into the seminary."

"I can't picture you doing any of that. I'm sure you'd be good at any profession you chose, but you can only be yourself. Who God meant you to be." She lowered her gaze and stared hard at the table's surface between them. "At least, that's what my older sister keeps telling me."

"She's right."

He considered the woman across from him, with her blond hair windblown and going every which way. She was lovelier every time he saw her. Today her cheeks were slightly flushed from what he guessed to be a busy day. She had that breathless look about her. Her words had been rolling around in his head all day. *It's an iron-clad, non-negotiable no-man, no-dating policy.*

He couldn't give up hope completely. Business first. And when the renovation was done, then he'd see where he stood with her.

At that exact moment her cell rang. She checked it and turned it off. "It's Aubrey. Food's served. I'm sorry, but I'm starving."

He stood to help her with her chair. "You'll stop by tomorrow when I'm there so I can show you what I have in mind?"

"I can do that."

"No more drive-by bakings?"

"Now, I can't promise that." She swished away.

She was so small and fragile, so whimsical and feminine, that a vibrant, steel-like emotion came to life in his heart, overtaking him. He watched her go with a mix of care and affection. He really liked her.

She stopped at the end of the row of tables. "Oh, I forgot to ask about the muffins. Did the men like them?"

"The monsters were the hit of the day."

She flashed him her brightest smile, the one that showed her dazzling spirit. The one that caught his heart like a hook on a line and dug deep. The hook did not leave as she walked away with her gait snapping and her golden hair swaying across her back. Even when she was out of his sight it remained, inexplicably.

Without Brice Donovan anywhere around, it was like a thousand times easier to remember her policy. Later that day, Ava jammed her Bible study materials into her tote and heaved it off the floor. The classroom in the church's auxiliary building was pleasant and serene, but then she always felt peaceful after spending an hour in fellowship, studying her Bible. She was focused and calm and everything seemed clear.

Aubrey fell in beside her and they trailed the small crowd filing out the door. "I'm in the mood for chocolate. Want to stop by the ice creamery and pig out on sundaes?"

"Like I would ever think that was a bad idea." Really. Did Aubrey even have to ask? She staggered under the weight of her mammoth bag. She was really going to have to find the time to go through it and clean it out—not that she was skilled at stuff like that. "I need sustenance if I'm going to be able to face my day tomorrow. It's jam-packed."

"You remembered we were going to babysit for Danielle, right?" Aubrey waited a beat before rolling her eyes. Their stepsister was happily married with two great kids. "It's okay. Don't even bother. I'll babysit and you'll do it next Friday. I've got that church retreat thing. So, tomorrow's packed?"

"It's just that I got this referral from Chloe's wedding. It was Brice, really—"

"Ex-boyfriend alert," Aubrey cut in, although by the interested lift of her eyebrows she'd caught the Brice reference. "It's Mike, directly ahead, in the hall."

They were still safely stuck in doorway of the classroom, in a small queue, but she was definitely visible. Ava could feel his smug gaze sweeping over her. She didn't have to look to know he had some poor clueless woman hanging on his arm. Two years ago, she'd been there, believing the stories he told about what a moral Christian guy he was on the surface.

Unfortunately, his supposed values were pure fabrication, and every time she spotted him she felt beyond foolish. Yep, even years later, her nose was turning glowing strawberry red again. Why couldn't she have noticed right away that he wasn't what he seemed? It was her fault-blindness. She just couldn't see the big glaring signs of trouble that other people could.

"That poor woman," Aubrey said with sympathy and kindness. Good, gentle Aubrey never made a fool of herself and never made any mistakes at all, much less mistakes of gargantuan proportion. "I'm going to add both of them to my prayers. She's bound to be heartbroken one day."

Just like I was. Ava could still feel the crack in her heart from him. "I'll pray for her, too."

She purposely didn't look ahead down the hall, so she wouldn't have to see him. Or to remember she'd really fallen hard for Mike. Discovering who he really was had been tough.

"And there's Ken." Aubrey grabbed Ava's wrist and steered her toward the far wall. "No, don't look up."

Great. Ken was probably with someone, too. He'd been the chef who, on the third date, said he'd waited long enough and tried to take liberties. She'd accidentally broken two fingers on his right hand when she'd bolted from the passenger seat of his car and slammed his hand in the door.

Really, did she look like the kind of girl who said one thing and did another?

No—it was some men. See? It went right back to them. They needed to think faithful, pious thoughts. Study their Bibles even more. She was really starting to get disillusioned about men. *All men.*

What about Brice? a little voice asked—a voice that seemed to come straight from her heart.

What about him? So, he'd been a gentleman so far, but wasn't that the problem? How deep did the gentleman thing go? She'd been fooled too many times by how a man *seemed.* So, he was Mr. Eligible Bachelor. Did that mean he was really good at fooling others? Or was he truly a good man, soul-deep?

Well, if she was interested in him, maybe that was a sign right there. Ken and Mike were excellent examples of her flaw-blindness. What if she was doing the same exact thing with Brice? If the man was interested in her, as time had proved over and over again, there had to be something wrong with him.

It was as simple as that. And if the tiny hope in her heart wished for more, that he truly was what he seemed, did she risk finding out? Face it, she didn't have Aubrey's quiet beauty or her sister Katherine's classic poise. She'd driven her own mother away.

Don't think about that. She squeezed the pain

from her heart. Erased the thought from her mind. Purposefully turned her thoughts from her failures and to her business. Her shop. She had more sketching to do tonight when they got home. And breakfast treats to bake for the construction dudes.

Maybe she'd do a batch of scones. She'd lose herself in the kitchen. Baking always made everything right. Baking made her problems and failures turn from shouts into silence.

There would be no dreaming. She'd lost too many dreams to waste them on what could never truly be. Brice had given her the perfect solution. He'd said he was happy to be friends. He didn't want anything to complicate their business relationship, and she was going to hold him to it, whether her heart liked it or not.

Pleased with that plan, she led Aubrey out of the church hall and through the parking lot, beeped the SUV unlocked and headed straight to the ice creamery.

Chapter Seven

Brice climbed out of his truck and into the morning. The hiss of the sprinkler system in the city park diagonally across the street provided enough background noise to drown out the faint hum of distant traffic. It was early enough yet that only an infrequent car motored down the nearby street. Birds took flight from the tree overhead when Rex hopped onto the sun-warmed blacktop. The parking lot was empty, except for them. He'd beat Ava here. Again.

Ava. Spotting her in the restaurant last night had given him a chance to clear the air. The only problem was, nothing felt clearer. Their agreement to keep it to business, sure, that was crystal clear. But his feelings for her became more complicated every time he was around her.

Lord, You know I'm in over my head. Please, I

need some help. If it's not too much trouble, show me the way.

As if in answer, he felt a shift in the calm peace of the morning. It was as if the nearly non-existent breeze had completely vanished, as if the world stopped spinning on its axis. As if for one nanosecond, the rotation of the earth ceased. Brice felt an odd prickling at the back of his neck. When he turned around, there she was.

Or, more accurately, there she was in her yellow SUV driving straight toward him. The morning light cut at an angle through her windshield, illumining her clearly. Those sunglasses were perched on her nose again, and the bill of the baseball cap—pink, today—framed her heart-shaped face. She whipped into the parking space closest to the front door. Right beside his truck.

Her nearness was like taking an unexpected punch to the chest. Brice rocked back on his heels from the impact. He watched her through the windshield as she chattered on her cell while cutting the engine, pulling the e-brake and gathering up her things.

Knowing there would be more bakery boxes and careens of coffee and spiced tea, he moved to help. Rex bounded ahead, whining in anticipation of being with Ava.

"I know just how you feel, buddy." He scrubbed his dog's head with his knuckles.

Her driver's side door was open, but she'd turned away, still busy gathering her things and absorbed in her phone conversation. Her dulcet, cheerful tone was as soft as the morning breeze. "Yes, Madeline, I'd be happy to bring by my catalogue. If your client wants something unique, then I'm the right baker. I specialize in one-of-a-kind designs."

She backed out of the vehicle, dragging her enormous purse with her. The bulk of it clattered over the console and snagged on the emergency brake, which stopped her progress. No one was cuter. Captivated, he could not look away as she freed her bag from the snag. Once it was free, she hooked the big bag over her shoulder, absently, and went to slam the door. With the keys inside.

Suddenly it wasn't a mystery how she kept locking herself out. He caught the edge of the door.

"Goodbye, Madeline and—" She stopped, apparently startled to find him latched onto her door. For the tiniest part of a millisecond she gazed up at him unguarded, forgetting to finish her conversation. "Uh…thanks again, Madeline, for this opportunity. I won't let you down. Bye!"

She snapped her phone shut. "Thank you, too. You keep showing up right when I need rescuing."

"It's a knack of mine." He waited for her to step out of the way before he settled behind the steering wheel and snagged the keys from the ignition. He started fiddling with the remote.

"And now what are you doing?"

"Reprogramming this for you. So it won't auto lock. There."

He was starting to look more and more like a fictitious knight in shining armor…well, more like a knight with a tool belt. It was nice to be rescued by such a good guy.

"Who was on the phone?" he asked over a few electronic beeps that came from inside the SUV.

"That was Madeline from Madeline's Catering. She provided the food for your sister's wedding reception. She asked me to make the desserts for a baby shower she's catering. The funniest thing, though. She said you had highly recommended me."

"I might have." He angled out from behind the wheel and closed the door.

"Thank you. I met with Maxime Frost yesterday, and her daughter Carly chose one of my designs. Also because of your recommendation."

"I'm just glad it worked out. If you want to head in, I'll bring in the boxes. Take a look at the plans. They're on the work table."

"Oh. Well, okay." Ava tried so hard not to like Brice more, but found it impossible. Fighting her feelings, she accepted Rex's good morning jump up, hugged him and promised him his own scone. Thrilled, his doggy tongue hanging, he bounded ahead of her on the way to the front door as if to say, hurry, faster!

"It's too bad I really don't like your dog," she said, not quite comfortable saying the truth, of how very much she adored Rex.

"Yeah, I don't like him either," Brice said with a wink.

She ducked her head to dig for her office keys in the mess of her bag. Truth was, she didn't want to keep looking at Brice. And see more and more good things to like about him. But her attempts were futile. There was Brice's reflection in the glass as she went to unlock the door.

My, he was such a fine man. Her heart gave a little tumble—just the tiniest fall.

It's just business. That's all. That's what it had to be.

So, why didn't that rationale feel convincing? Best not to think about that too much. She pushed open the door. Rex sprung in, expertly dodging the sawhorses and piles of fresh wallboard, and she lingered, turning to watch Brice. It was hard not to notice the powerful agile way he hefted the boxes, shut the back of the SUV and locked up.

He was a great guy—wait, rephrase that. He was a really awesome man. Why did that make her panic?

"It's starting to take shape." His voice and his boots echoed in the big empty shop. "You can see we've got the rewiring done. The inspector's supposed to be here in an hour. Once we get that okayed, the wallboard goes up. Do you like the cathedral ceilings? We were able to punch up a few feet higher than we'd first thought."

See? Just business. Ava managed to push aside

the lump of feelings all wadded up in her chest. Did her best not to notice how she felt happy when he was near.

"I love the ceilings. It's better than I hoped for." She walked around, giving Brice time to head into the kitchen with the mornings treats, and to put space between them. "The guys have done a great job."

She could see her dreams of the new shop taking shape in the shell of the old. She'd have warm honeyed woods, cheerful yellow walls and the scent of happiness in the air. It was finally happening. For real. She thought of Madeline's call—was it a sign her business would boom? Maybe.

She had a business to build, not more mistakes to make. She caught sight of Brice unboxing the scones. A tiny question whispered inside her heart: What if he wasn't a mistake?

"Ava, you've topped yourself." He had one of the sunshine face scones in hand.

"I made a double batch, so the construction dudes can take some home to their families."

"Once you get this shop open, I hope you know that you're going to be in demand."

"From your lips to God's ears," she said, trying to stay focused on the business. The business. Not on Brice's kind words.

He took a bite. "Sheer heaven. You'll be open soon. Do you have hired help all lined up?"

"Are you kidding? I've got enough extended

family to hire without even putting an ad in the paper. I'm just hoping this doesn't wind up being another failure."

"It won't be." Brice could see the burden of it weighing her down. "You have an excellent quality of product, and the decorating is top notch. It's all I heard at Chloe's reception. I think you should believe in yourself a little more. It will turn out fine."

"You're just saying that to be nice, mister."

"That's the idea. I want to be nice to you. This is business, remember? We have this business relationship, but after that, I'm hoping you'll want more."

"Oh, that's scarier than starting my own business." She swiped a lock of golden hair out of her eyes, looking adorable. "It's that fault-blind thing. You look perfect to me, but it's just because I can't see the flaws. It's like walking blind into a tornado."

"Good. No man wants you to see his flaws."

"Some people are better at hiding them than others." She followed him into the kitchen where sunlight highlighted the drawings he'd set out beside the bakery box. "Take me, my flaws are totally noticeable."

"I haven't noticed any flaws."

"Sure you haven't. What about those accusations?"

"Those were perfectly understandable considering you were confusing me with a Darren Fullerton."

Really, he was just trying to get her to like him, and it wasn't going to work. Absolutely not. The same way she *wasn't* going to notice how wonderfully tall he was. Solid. Substantial. How he looked like a man who could shoulder any burden. Solve any problem.

Okay, she was starting to notice, but only just a little. Really.

Rex, the perfect gentleman, was sitting there with his big innocent eyes showing just how good and deserving he was of a scone. Ava turned her attention to the dog because there was no reason why she shouldn't fall in love with Rex. She grabbed one of the cheerful iced treats. "Here you go, handsome."

Rex delicately took the scone from her fingertips, gave her a totally adoring look and sucked the sweet down in one gulp.

"He seems to like your baking," Brice said with a grin. "Can you stay for a while? I can pour you a cup of coffee if you want to look over the—"

"Oh." She was already looking at the drawings, and it was her turn to be utterly adoring. She couldn't believe her eyes. Could she talk? No. The penciled images had stolen every word from her brain. Her mind was a total blank except for a single thought.

Perfect.

He'd taken the photos she'd showed him yesterday and transformed them into her vision. Into exactly what she'd imagined. There it was. Curlicue scrollwork and rosebud-patterned moldings and carvings framing the wood and glass bakery case. "There's no way I can afford this."

"Custom woodwork is built into the estimate you signed. This would be for the same price. We've agreed to it."

"How can that be? I love this, don't get me wrong, but this can't be what was on the estimate. I know it's not."

"Rafe doesn't do woodwork, so pricing it is a mystery to him. Trust me. I can do this for the same price as he quoted you."

"Are you sure?"

"Positive. There's no hidden costs and no hidden agendas. With me, what you see is what you get."

"Business-wise, right?"

"Always."

She loved the sincerity in his words. The honesty he projected was totally irresistible. Now she *had* to like him. But just a pinch. A smidgeon. But not a drop more.

"I love this." She traced the drawn image of the bakery case with her fingertips. "This is my dream."

"That was the idea." He leaned closer to study the drawing, too, and to set a coffee cup in front of her. The steely curve of his upper arm brushed against her shoulder and stayed.

The trouble was, she noticed. She liked being close to him. She felt safe and secure and peaceful, as if everything was right in the world.

"If I have your approval, then I'll get started in the wood shop today. On one condition."

"Name it."

"Send two dozen of these scones to my office along with the bill." He moved away to take another treat from the box and broke it in half. Tossed one piece to the dog, who caught it like a pro ballplayer, and kept the other for himself. "Do you deliver?"

"For you, I could make an exception."

"Excellent. It's a pleasure doing business with you, Miss McKaslin."

"Anytime, Mr. Donovan." It was a good thing she had her priorities straight in life. Because otherwise, she could completely fall for him. Talk about doom!

She pushed away from the table, away from his presence and away from the wish of what could be. She grabbed her cup of coffee. "Later, Donovan."

"Later, McKaslin."

She gave Rex a pat and sauntered out of her shop like a businesswoman totally in charge of her life and her heart.

It was a complete facade.

Rex's high yelping rose above the grind of the radial saw. Brice slipped down his protective glasses and glanced over his shoulder toward the open workshop door.

Maura, his secretary, had walked the twenty or so yards from the front office and stood staring at him, her arms crossed over her chest, looking like a middle-aged spinster despite the fact that they'd gone through public school together. "The scones you ordered are here. Talk about amazing. We're all taking a coffee break. You want to come join us?"

"Ava was here?" He hadn't expected her to be by so fast. He'd figured she would have to make another batch, but she must have made enough originally. He hadn't planned on that, he'd been busy working on her molding and now he'd missed her.

Maura shrugged. "I didn't know you wanted to see her. I'll make sure she doesn't run off next time."

She gave him that smile that women have, the knowing one that means you aren't fooling them one bit, and he was floored. Just how many people had guessed about his feelings for Ava?

"I've heard her cakes are heavenly." Maura paused in the doorway, giving that smile again. "When you order next time, remember—we all love chocolate. Don't forget, now."

"It's a business relationship." It was the truth. For now. "What makes you think it isn't?"

Maura arched one brow and stared pointedly at the pile of wood. "You always take the summer months off, but it's now June and look, you're still here. You aren't fooling me. And for your 4-1-1, she's really nice. She goes to my church and we're in the same Bible study. I could put in a good word for you."

"I can handle it, thanks."

"It's just that I know what happened with Whitney. It wasn't your fault." Maura kindly didn't say more on that topic. "I hope you know what you're doing. You haven't dated in a long time."

"Thanks, Maura, but I have a plan."

"Well, if you need a woman's opinion, you can always run it by me." She hesitated again. "Thanks for the scones. They are wonderful." And finally she was gone, shutting the door tight behind her.

A plan? That wasn't what he'd thought to call it before now. He lifted the length of wood from the bench, a smooth piece of oak that would gleam like honey when he was through with it. He had a plan, of sorts. He intended to work hard. To deliver on his promise to Ava. To show her that he could help her with this dream. Maybe—God willing—with all her dreams.

The problem was, he didn't know if he could get her to go to dinner with him. It wasn't looking promising at this moment in time.

Based on his experience with her so far, he feared that Ava McKaslin might be the Mt. Everest equivalent of dating—a nearly impossible feat to accomplish and not for the faint of heart. A smart man would choose a much smaller mountain that required less effort.

He, apparently, wasn't a smart man, but he was a dedicated one and he recognized her value. He set his goggles in place, grabbed another length of oak from the lumber pile. He had long hours of detail-

ing to do and he intended to bring this in on time.
He'd work on this dream first.

Then he'd try to tackle the rest of them.

Chapter Eight

In the serenity of her oldest sister's snazzy kitchen, Ava piped careful scrollwork across the final dozen cookies in the shape of a baby's shoe. Madeline, the caterer, had subcontracted with her for six dozen specialty cookies for a baby shower and they were going perfectly. It was a good feeling, a relieved feeling. The first she'd had in two days. That's how long she'd gone without seeing Brice.

You'd think that would be enough time to get her feelings under control, right? But no, she thought as she piped the final curlicue on the last cookie and stretched her aching back. She had feelings for him, and she liked him. But that didn't mean she had to actually do anything about it, right?

She'd been avoiding seeing him. Oh, she'd continued to deliver baked goods for the construction dudes, but she arrived way early, well before Brice was supposed to show, and just left the box in the kitchen. *Drive-by baking,* as he'd called it.

She hit the Off button on her digital music player and plucked the buds from her ears just in time. Katherine was tapping down the hall, coming her way. Since she was in big, deep favor-debt to her sister, Ava snatched a ceramic mug from the cabinet and poured a brisk cup of tea she'd had ready, steeping. The instant Katherine stepped foot in the kitchen, she had the cup on the breakfast bar and was heating a monster muffin in the microwave.

"Wow, it smells amazing in here." Dressed in a modest summer dress and sensible flat sandals, Katherine slid onto a breakfast bar stool. The classy act that she was, she didn't even comment on the shambles of her ordinarily super-tidy kitchen. "These cookies are too beautiful to eat. Your customer will be delighted, I'm sure."

Talk about a great sister. Ava rescued the muffin from the microwave and set it next to the tea. "Ta da! I promise I'll have this place spic-and-span by the time you get home today."

"I'm not worried about it in the slightest."

Katherine had so much faith in her, sometimes it was hard to get past the fear of letting her down. Ava went back to her cookies, boxing the ones that were ready, leaving the others to dry a few more minutes. The icing was still a tad tacky. Out of the corner of her eye she watched her sister bow her head and whisper a blessing over the meal. Her mammoth engagement diamond glinted in the overhead lights.

Katherine hadn't had the easiest time with things, but she'd made a success of her life. She'd become such a graceful woman. It was no wonder at all why she'd found a good man to fall love with her and promise her the real thing—true love—for a lifetime to come.

Katherine was the kind of lady true love happened to. Ava laid a sheet of waxed paper across the first layer of cookies in the box, not at all sure that true love would ever happen to her personally. She loved the dream, but all she had to do was to think of the long string of romantic disasters lying behind her like a desolate wasteland, and she knew, soul deep, it wasn't possible for her.

Or was it? Brice liked her. He had from the very start. Like he was either desperate, or maybe—*maybe*—this could be the start of something extraordinary. Something rare. Because she had to admit, what she felt for him was simply unusual. She had gotten to know him more, and he was a great guy—not just on the outside. He had a big heart, was an honorable character. He could see her dreams.

But was that enough to risk amending her no-dating policy? *That* was the million-dollar question.

"I love these." Katherine studied the muffin she'd bitten into. "Are you going to put these in your bakery? You'll have people beating down the door for them."

"From your lips to God's ears. Wouldn't that be something, if I actually succeeded at this? I've got a bunch of leftover muffins. Do you want to take some to the store? Maybe the early morning customers would like a muffin break."

"That'd be perfect. We have a reader's group this morning."

"Oh, and I've got the last of the cake sketches done. Do you want to see them now?"

"Are you kidding? Show me what you've got, sweetie."

Ava hauled out her mammoth sketch pad and removed the soft, pastel-colored drawings from the front. "I know you're going with a roses theme. Pinks and ivory. So I went with that."

She slid the drawings one by one onto the breakfast bar, carefully watching her sister's face for signs of dismay and abhorrence, but there was only a happy gasp of delight.

"Ava, these are so wonderful! I'm never going to be able to choose between them."

Whew. What a relief. The last thing she ever wanted to do was to disappoint her sister. Her family was all she had, and she loved them so much. "If you can't choose, maybe I should do a few more sketches. The right design should just jump out at you. It's something your heart decides."

"No, sweetie, you misunderstand. I feel that way about each one these. I love this rose garden theme. Can you really do this with frosting?"

"It's easy."

"I'm going to show these to Jack and see what he has to say. But…oh, the golden climbing roses on this ivory cake, with the leaves, that's stunning too."

"I can amend any of this, too. That's not carved in stone, you know. A little erasing and redrawing and *ta da*, the wedding cake of your dreams."

Katherine gathered up the sketches with care. "Are you okay? You seem a little down this morning."

"Down? No, not me. I'm always in a good mood." As long as she didn't think about Brice, that is. She moved away—quick—before Katherine figured it out, and started assembling a second bakery box. "I've got a lot on my mind. The renovation is stressful."

"I've heard nothing but renovation horror stories. What problems are you having?"

Katherine was watching her carefully over the rim of her teacup, so Ava did her best to steer the topic away from her confused, tangled up heart. "None. Not a single problem. The construction workers are organized. They've got their schedule, they do their work on time, they've already got the inspectors lined up, so there's hardly any downtime. I haven't been by yet, but they are supposed to have all the wallboard up and taped. Can you believe it? My shop is going to have brand new pretty walls and wiring that's up to code."

"I'm thrilled for you."

"I should be able to open on time. Danielle is going to help me set up my books. I've been throwing all my receipts into a shoebox in my closet. That's not going to work for a long-term bookkeeping solution, or so she tells me."

"No, sorry." Katherine smiled in that gentle, caring way of hers. "Now, tell me the truth. Something's bothering you. Is it the stress of getting a start-up business off the ground? You know you have us to help."

Ava nodded, slipping the last of the cookies into the box and snapping shut the lid. She deftly avoided mentioning her romantic confusion. "Tell Spence I might be a little late for my shift this afternoon. I have an ad to put into the church bulletin. The deadline's today. Oh, and I'm meeting Danielle for a bookkeeping session."

"Sure." She kept sipping her tea, assessing over the rim.

Ava knew what was coming. "Well, I've got a busy morning. See you—"

"Wait a minute. Don't run off just yet. You haven't told me what's wrong." Katherine was a sharp tack. "That leaves only one possibility left. You like Brice Donovan, don't you?"

"*Like?* That's a pretty strong word. Especially for a woman who has a brilliant no-dating policy." The smartest thing she'd ever done, hands down. Because without it, she'd be letting Brice charm her. Letting him close. Letting him into her heart.

"I know you just want me to be happy, but I'm nothing but a country love song gone wrong."

"There's not one thing wrong with you. Maybe with some of the men you've spent time with, but you made the right decision in the end. Besides, you can't really get to know a man—any man, good or not so good—unless you spend time with him and get to know what he's really like."

That was the problem with Katherine. She always saw the good side. She believed that good things happened to good people, but she just didn't see the truth. Good men happened to *other* women, not her.

"Says the happily engaged woman. Get back to me on those sketches, right?" She grabbed the cookie box and her keys. If she left fast enough, Katherine couldn't say—

"Not every man is going to leave you, Ava. Not every man is going to let you down."

Too late. Ava stopped dead in her tracks, with her hand on the garage door. "I'm not going to give any man a chance to. I'll see you later, alligator."

Katherine said nothing, nothing at all, not that Ava gave her much of a chance to. She'd practically leaped into the garage and closed the inner door after her. Trying to shove out the words echoing in her head. *Not every man is going to leave you, Ava. Not every man is going to let you down*

And Brice's words, *With me, what you see is what you get.*

Business wise, right? she'd asked.

Always.

Would believing in him be the right thing? Heart pounding, she caught her breath in the echoing garage, feeling the pieces of her past rain down on her like soot and ash, willing away the sadness. It came anyway. Sharp and bone-deep and in her mother's voice.

Why, after all these years, did she still feel like that seven-year-old girl, standing in their old backyard beneath the snap of the clothes drying on the line, watching the blur of their 1960s Ford disappear down the alley? Why did she still feel the panic of being to blame? Why did it feel as if every failure just added to that pain?

She'd prayed for as long as she could remember with every fiber of her being for a good man to come into her life. But unlike all her other prayers, that one had remained unanswered. Over the years, her wishes had faded in luster and possibility until she couldn't see them anymore.

And she was better off that way, really. Her no-man policy had been working perfectly fine. She'd already taken the leap to start a business. Already bought a shop and had placed advertisements, and already word-of-mouth recommendations were starting to come in. Okay, people weren't exactly knocking down her door, but it was a start, right?

She'd finally learned to stop spending her life with her head in the clouds and now what?

Brice.

She'd finally stopped looking for the one man whose heart was stalwart enough to love her through all time and accepted that he didn't exist. At least, not for her. And then what?

Brice. He came into her life like the impossible dream she'd given up on. But was he so impossible?

"Ava? Hel-*lo?* Earth to Ava." Aubrey slowed the SUV to a crawl. "You've been a space cadet all day."

"I know. Sorry." Ava blinked, focusing. She'd been trying to think of everything but Brice all day, and what was she doing? Looking out the window to see if his pickup was in her shop's parking lot. Pathetic, she thought, undoing her seat belt. It looked as if the coast was clear. "Just park here at the curb."

"Are you kidding? I'm coming, too. I've been dying to see this all week." Aubrey cut the engine and pulled the e-brake. She never forgot to remove the keys. "Just think, this time next week it will be done. Can you believe it?"

"No. Yes. I don't have to be too terrified of this venture failing until I open the doors, officially, for business." It wasn't the business she was terrified of, at the moment, but of not seeing Brice. Of turning down his more-than-friends offer to date, after the shop was done.

"You won't fail," Aubrey said with confidence. "You don't give yourself enough credit."

What did she say to that? Ava stumbled out into the stifling heat. The temperature was in the high nineties, and heat radiated off the pavement. She had to stop and dig through her purse to find her keys, no small feat. It gave her plenty of time to think over Aubrey's words.

She gave herself plenty of credit. But what did you do when you succeeded at attracting doom? Most of the time, she didn't let it bother her, but now....

Now, it was Brice. She could really fall for him, harder than any man she'd ever known. And that meant her heart could really be broken, right?

"Let me." Aubrey grabbed Ava's bag, plunged her hand in and pulled out the wallet so thick with debit and credit card receipts that it wouldn't snap shut. "There they are—at the bottom."

"I keep meaning to clean this bag out."

"I know." Aubrey dumped the wallet, papers and all, back into the bag and unlocked the door. She looked around the inside of the shop. "Wow, this looks *great*."

"Wow. It does." Ava followed her sister inside. The cooled air washed over her as she stared in awe at the tall cathedral ceilings and real walls. All the mess had been cleaned up. The cement slab was perfectly swept. The taped and mudded wallboard wasn't pretty, but it took no imagination at all to add paint and trim and flooring to see the airy, sunny result.

Footsteps boomed in the kitchen behind them. Heavy, booted steps. Ava heard her sister yelp, felt

Aubrey's instant fear, but she *knew* the sound and rhythm of that gait. The instant she'd stepped foot into the building, she should have recognized his presence.

"Your dream is taking shape." Brice Donovan filled the threshold between the kitchen and the main room looking like her dream come true in a simple black T-shirt, black jeans and boots. He looked stalwart and easygoing, like a guy a girl could always depend on.

Her heart wished for him a tiny bit more. It was a sweet twist of pain that moved through her. She stepped toward him and her spirit brightened. "Your construction guys have done a wonderful job. It's just right."

"The finish work starts Monday. We'll be done before you know it."

She gulped, unable to speak. There was only the magnetic draw of his gaze. Of his dimpled grin. Of his presence that drew her like an unsuspecting galaxy toward a black hole. That couldn't be a good thing, could it?

"This must be your sister." Brice broke his gaze, releasing her, to hold out his hand to her sister. "It's good to meet you."

"Ava hasn't said a word about me, has she?" Aubrey's hand looked engulfed by Brice's larger one.

Oh, no. Ava held her breath, sensing what would come next. Knowing that, like it or not, Aubrey would *know.* It was that twin thing. Their brain cells would fire and she would guess the horrible secret Ava was keeping from everyone, including herself.

Yep, there it was. In the change in Aubrey's jaw line, her stance, her voice. Aubrey withdrew her hand, but there was an "ah ha" glint in her eyes. "I know why she hasn't said anything about you. In fact, she's refused to do a whole lot of talking about this very important renovation."

"It's all the stress," Ava added. The stress of the construction, the financing, getting a new business started, of being afraid she was falling in deep like with a man who was entirely wrong for her.

"I understand completely." The way Brice said it, it was like he had unauthorized access to that twin brain cell, and that was impossible. "Ava and I currently have a business-only policy."

"Ah, so that explains it," Aubrey said as she backed toward the door. "I'm probably just in the way here. Brice, you probably have a lot of construction things to go over with Ava."

"As a matter of fact, I do have a few things to show her."

"Oh, *sure* you do." Ava couldn't believe it. That didn't sound very business-like. She narrowed her eyes at him. "Why are you here, anyway?"

"I spent all day in the woodshop, and I wanted to stop by and see the progress for myself. Make sure nothing had been overlooked before the painters show up at seven Monday morning. I want this done right for you."

When he smiled, she couldn't stop the rise of her spirit, the tug of longing in her heart. She'd come by because she'd wanted to see the progress of her dream, and Aubrey had wanted to see it, too. Now Aubrey was at the door, tugging it open. What kind of world was this when your twin abandoned you? Panic rattled through her. She'd feel better if Aubrey would stay—

"Aubrey, why don't you stay with us?" Brice asked. "Unless you two have other plans?"

"Not at all," Aubrey said so fast. "None that can't be changed. We were just going to barbecue supper."

"*What?* Wait one minute." Ava had a bad feeling about this. It was four-thirty on a Saturday afternoon. Not exactly business hours. "Brice and I have a strict policy to adhere to."

"True. But we agreed to excuse dating and romance from our business policy, right? That doesn't mean we can't be friends."

"Friends." Friendship did not begin to describe this swirl of confusing emotions she had for him. Emotions she did not want to analyze, thank you very much. What she wanted to do was to stay in denial about them. Denial was an excellent coping method.

"Sure, my business partner has been my best friend since kindergarten. Friendship and business don't have to be mutually exclusive. In fact, it can often be beneficial. If you two don't mind, come out to my place. I fix a mean steak. I was going to barbecue dinner tonight anyway, I'll just throw a few more steaks and shrimp on the barbie—"

"Shrimp?" Aubrey perked up.

Now there was no way to get out of this. Ava knew she *should* be sensible, like her sister Katherine. Stoic and self-disciplined like big brother Spence. Be calm and think things through like her twin. Her problems always came from leaping before she looked, and right now looking at his dark tousle of hair, the curve of his grin and the steady hope in his eyes made her want to leap into agreement.

"Lots of shrimp," Brice promised. "I've got a shop behind my garage, so I work at home a lot when I'm doing custom stuff like this. Hey, while you two are there, I'll show you a few new ideas I have. Something for the display case."

"Now I don't believe there's an allowance for even more custom stuff in the contract I signed."

"True. This is just because. This is what I want to do for you as a friend. We start as friends. See where it goes from there."

Didn't that sound harmless? It was like a test-drive of a new car. You got to see if you liked it first before you bought it. It was the same situation here. If she didn't like him for a friend, she wouldn't date him and marry him, right?

Ava felt her heart fall even more. There it was, that terrible urge to leap. To just tell him yes. Friends first, and then let's see where this goes. What could go wrong with that?

Chapter Nine

"Did you know he lived up here?" Aubrey asked from behind the wheel as she negotiated the curving road that led into the foothills where the posh people lived.

"Nope. I had no clue."

Ava couldn't seem *not* to look at Brice. There he was right in front of them in his snazzy red sports car.

Aubrey followed Brice into an exclusive gated community. "If you're falling for this guy, you have to stop this destructive thing you do."

"I tried my best at all my other relationships. It's my fault-blindness. Maybe it's a good thing you're here. I need your help. You can watch for his faults that I can't see."

"You *definitely* need help." Aubrey rolled her eyes and turned her full attention back to the road.

"Look at this place. This is really wow. How rich is this guy?"

"He's a Donovan. How rich are they?"

"Well, his grandfather knew Grandpop. They played golf together."

Grandpop had been pretty rich. "It still hurts to think about him, doesn't it?"

"Yeah." Aubrey paused a moment, the sadness settling between them. He'd been gone two years now and it was a terrible hole in the family. It was why Gran had moved permanently to their winter home in Scottsdale. She'd found it so painful to be alone in the house he built for her when they were a young married couple, that she simply stayed down south where there were fewer memories to haunt her.

The quiet stayed between them as they followed Brice through a gate and along a grand driveway to a private house tucked into the hill, surrounded by lush trees and lawn. Views of the Bridger Mountains backed up behind him, and views of the Rockies rimmed the entire western exposure.

Brice parked in the third bay of a three-car garage, and Ava was too busy looking around to realize Aubrey had parked the SUV and was already climbing out of the vehicle. Okay, pay attention. She joined her sister outside the wood and stone house that looked like something out of a magazine.

"That's nicer than Gran's house," Aubrey said.

True. Which only pointed out the plain truth.

Brice was so wrong for her. He was going to look for the wife to fit into this house. Face it. It was such a good thing they had this friends-only policy.

He closed the car door and pocketed his keys. "C'mon in this way. I never use the front door."

"Not even when you entertain?" Aubrey asked.

"I never entertain. Having my folks over is about as elaborate as I get." There was that grin again, the inviting warmth, the good-guy charm that was so totally arresting.

He held open the door for them at the back of the garage. Ava saw a wide but short hallway with a laundry room to her right elbow and what had to be a huge pantry to her left. Ahead of her was an enormous kitchen with a family room off to the side, not that she noticed that. She was too busy salivating over the kitchen.

Gleaming, light maple cabinets and a gray granite countertop stretched for miles. She spotted a gas range, Sub-Zero refrigerator and a double oven. There were plenty of windows, a bay in a huge eating nook and then a row of them looking out to the green backyard. "This is better than Katherine's kitchen."

Brice went straight to the fridge. "Is that where you've been doing your baking?"

"Yeah. It's working out okay, but sometimes I know I'm in her way." Ava ran her hand over the expensive granite. "This is a nice work space you've got here."

"It's wasted on me. I don't cook much. What do you want to drink? I've got soda, iced tea and lemonade. Oh, and milk." He opened the door wide so she could see what was on the shelves.

Something pink caught her eye. "Wait one minute. You have strawberry milk?"

"Chocolate, too."

"I never would have pegged you for a guy who would drink pink milk."

"Hey, I like strawberries. Nothing wrong with that."

"No, it's just—" Did she tell him it was one of her very favorite things? "I'll take a glass of pink milk. Aubrey will, too."

"Do you always speak for her?"

"I'm just trying to be efficient. Where are your glasses?"

"Sit down. Both of you. You're guests, let me do the fetching." His words were deceptively light but when his gaze raked over her, tenderness charged the air between them.

Hmm. That didn't feel like friendship. It felt like "more than friendship" in the nicest way she'd ever experienced. She took a shaky breath. Whatever she did, she had to remember not to start reading things into his actions. *Friends only,* he'd said. But she knew he wanted more.

"Wow," Aubrey said somewhere behind her, and Ava turned.

"Look at that pool. It's bigger than Gran's."

Ava went weak in the knees. "There's my favorite guy."

Rex was lounging in the cooling spray of the pool fountain. He looked up with a start, gave a goofy grin and heaved himself up on all fours. Dripping wet he took off for a run and disappeared from sight around a huge sixteen-foot awning that shaded a patio set, chaise lounges and a built-in brick grill.

"Rex!" Brice called out a second before a big golden streak charged into the kitchen.

The sound of heavy dog breathing drew Ava's attention to the archway where the retriever streaked toward her. She caught a faint glimpse of a sleek dining room and a comfortable living room in the background before the oaf lunged toward her, both front feet wrapping around her shoulders. His tongue roughened her face and she started to laugh. The dripping heap of retriever stopped licking to give her a goofy grin and then started over again.

"Stop! Stop!" Ava was laughing, but it was kind of hard not to like such a good-hearted dog.

Out of the corner of her eye she saw Brice round the long span of counter, coming to her rescue, but it was too late. Rex dropped to the floor in front of her and gave a huge shake. Water droplets rained everywhere.

If she wasn't soaked enough down the front from his hug, she was now. The retriever dropped to his haunches looking from Brice's disapproving face to hers. Rex's eyebrows shot up, the goofy grin dropped from his cute face and the happiness faded from his chocolate-sweet eyes. His whine said, "Oh, no. I messed up again."

Ava's heart fell and she followed him to the floor where she wrapped her arms around Rex's wet neck. "I don't mind," she told him. "I know you didn't *mean* for disaster to happen."

"Speak for yourself," Aubrey commented on a laugh. "I was standing downwind and now I'm wet, too."

"But he was just excited." Ava kept one arm around the canine's neck. "I'm in love with this guy."

Rex gave a whine low in his throat and dropped his huge head on her shoulder.

"The feeling appears to be mutual." Brice. There he was, all six feet of solid male kneeling down, meeting her gaze with his. "Rex knows better than this. He just can't help himself sometimes."

"I think he's perfect."

"Another mutual sentiment."

Perfect, Brice thought, that's what Ava was. Dripping wet, her honey gold bangs tousled from wet dog kisses, sprayed with droplets, she'd never been more beautiful.

"I've always wanted a dog just like this, but Dad's allergic to dogs." She glowed with happiness as she hugged Rex, who looked like he was in heaven. "And then we've been in apartments and too busy for a pet. But one day, I want a handsome guy just like you."

Rex's eyes melted with adoration and gave Ava another swipe across the face.

"You are the best dog." She laughed, all spirit, all brightness and big loving heart.

Brice was enchanted. Tenderness blazed so strongly, it transformed him completely. His heart fell—a measureless, infinite tumble from which there was no return.

They were beneath the shady awning, seated at the poolside table with an impressive view of the sparkling azure water. Ava looked around, ignoring the full plate of food in front of her. The forest-like backyard and the rise of the Bridger Mountains spearing up to the sky were spectacular. She had to give Brice's home full marks.

But his cooking, wow. That deserved full marks plus. The juicy, flavorful steak was grilled to perfection. Talk about a total shocker. Who would have guessed that when Brice said he cooked a mean steak, he meant it?

He sat across the snazzy teak table, the breezes lazily ruffling his dark hair. He cut a strip off the fourth steak he'd barbecued—for Rex—and tossed it to him. Rex caught it neatly, gulped, swallowed and sat back down on his haunches.

The gentle waterfall of the fountain and the leaves rustling through the trees only added to the pleasantness of the evening.

Earlier, after readying the steaks in their

marinade, Brice had brought their glasses of strawberry milk to the poolside and relaxed in the shade.
Since their clothes were wet anyway, she and
Aubrey did cannonballs into the pool, trying to see
who could leave the biggest splash marks. Ava had
won, but it had been an intensely close—and fun—
competition.

Now, drying in the hundred-degree shade, she
was just still damp enough from the pool to be comfortable temperature wise. But emotionally? Not so
much. Brice dominated her field of vision. He was
impossible to ignore.

"I read in the paper a while back that you were
engaged," Aubrey said abruptly as she poked the
tines of her fork into a cube of red herbed potatoes
heaped on her plate. "Didn't the wedding get cancelled?"

What? Ava could not believe her ears. The fork
tumbled out of her hand and fell into the three-bean
salad. Hello? Aubrey did *not* just say that, did she?
How could she stick her nose where it didn't belong?

Brice winced as if he'd taken a painful blow.
"That's true. I was engaged to Whitney Phelps."

"Of the Butte Phelps," Aubrey nodded, as if
coaxing Brice along.

Ava sank into the comfy cushions of her chair
and felt as if a hundred-pound weight had settled
onto her chest. Sympathy filled her.

Brice put down his steak knife and took a long
pull of strawberry milk. "It was one of those things.

I'd just turned twenty-five. I had this plan. I had my business started and it was going well, and I was ready to get married. I figured we'd date for two years, get engaged for a year, be married for a couple more and then have kids."

"It sounds like a good plan to me," Aubrey said in the gentle quiet way of hers that made anybody want to tell her anything. "What happened?"

Ava knew. She could see it play across his face. Feel the resonance of it in his heart. He'd really loved this woman. The right way—heart deep and honestly. She wasn't surprised when he spoke.

"The moment I saw Whitney, I thought she was classy. Poised. Polished. Just what I was looking for." His tone wasn't bitter. There was no anger in his words. Nor was there any pining. Just the pain of regret. "I must have been what she was looking for, too."

"I imagine so," Aubrey answered.

Poor Whitney, Ava thought. She must have felt something like this. Overwhelmed by his million-dollar grin and honesty. Helplessly sucked in by the pull of those deep dark eyes. Enamored by his decency and strength and manliness. Lost in too many wishes to find her way out.

Brice stared down at his plate for a moment, as if gathering his thoughts. A muscle tightened in his square granite jaw. "We came from the same backgrounds. We seemed compatible. I cared for her, and she fit into my plan. Or, maybe I made her. I prayed for our relationship to work out. For it to progress. Sometimes I wonder if I imposed way too much too early when we were dating, instead of just trusting God to work things out for the best."

Oh, I so know what you mean. Ava felt the heavy pain radiate out from the center of her chest, into her throat, into her voice. "You have to be very careful what you pray for."

"Exactly." His gaze met hers, and she felt the connection, an emotional zing that opened her heart right up.

"I prayed," he said, "and while my prayers were answered in a way, I'll never know how much I messed up God's plan for me. Maybe He had someone better for me, a better match, and a better chance for happiness for both me and Whitney separately. I don't know."

I understand completely, Ava thought.

"I only know He answered my prayers, but I asked in the wrong way. Whitney and I would never have made each other happy in the end. It was hard, admitting that, because I cared for her deeply. I was a disappointment to her. She slowly became disappointed in me. These days when I pray, I ask for the Lord to show me the way He wants me to go."

You're not falling in total serious like with him, she commanded herself. She knew better than that. So, he was perfect in many ways. She could feel the weight of his pain and the honesty of his experience. Her heart tumbled a little more.

"It was a mess." He shrugged one big shoulder, looking vulnerable even for such a big, brawny guy. "My mom hasn't forgiven me completely for calling off the wedding. She was very attached to Whitney."

"Your mom still hasn't forgiven you?"

Brice studied Ava's dismay. "She'd come to love Whitney like a daughter and it was a severe loss for her. She loves me, but I'm different from my parents in a lot of ways. They just don't get me."

"You're talking about your construction company?"

"Yep. Like the dog. He's not a purebred." He cut another piece of steak for Rex. "Not that it's good or bad, I just was looking for a best buddy, and went to the pound looking for a puppy. Rex and me, we connected."

When his gaze met hers, Brice couldn't tell if she knew that's how he felt about her. There'd been something special about her right from the beginning, something unique and amazing and rare that made him look and keep looking.

And it kept him riveted now. She made him take this risky step toward another relationship. It was hard opening himself up. But he took the risk. "Ava, it's your turn to tell the real story behind your no-man policy."

"What? Oh, you so don't want to hear about that." Ava averted her eyes, dismissing his question. Then, as she cut a small bite off her steak, she appeared to reconsider. "Maybe it is a good idea. Then you can see what I mean and you'll understand how important being just friends is to me."

"Tell me."

"Where to start?" She looked to Aubrey for help.

Aubrey took a sip of strawberry milk. "The high-school boyfriend. It's classic Ava."

"True." Ava set down her fork, looking even more adorable with the way her hair was drying in a flyaway tangle. "Okay, here's the scoop. Lloyd was in my earth sciences class. Now, I'm totally not a science whiz but I had to take some kind of science credit, and it was like the easiest science class in our high school. So there I was, trying to figure out some weird earth crust layer experiment, I don't know, I never did figure it out. Lloyd was cute, he saw me struggling and came over to help me. I need a lot of help."

"I'm beginning to see that." Big time. She clearly could take care of herself, but it didn't hurt to have, say, someone like him to look out for her. Help her find her keys, watch over her, make her happy. He was interested in that job. "Poor Lloyd. I bet he fell for you."

"Poor Lloyd," Aubrey agreed with a nod.

Just what he'd thought. Brice could picture it. The teenage boy probably had such an incredible crush on Ava to begin with, he'd been all vulnerable heart. "What did poor Lloyd do that made you dump him?"

"Oh, it wasn't me," Ava insisted. "I liked him. I mean, he was cute."

"Cute," Aubrey agreed, a mirror of Ava. "But clueless."

"He was like a big dopey puppy, sorry, Rex." Ava flashed him a smile and the big adoring dog tilted his head to one side, quirked his brows and gave a sappy grin. Totally besotted.

Yeah, Brice knew just how he felt.

"A girl wants a boyfriend with a clue. Aubrey, what was the first really nutso thing Lloyd did?"

"The utility pole."

"That's right, our first date. We were on our way for hamburgers at the drive-in, and he drove smack into a big light pole going twenty-five miles an hour. Not looking where he was going." Ava lifted both hands in a helpless gesture. "He wouldn't stop looking at me while he was driving. I kept telling him to keep his eyes on the road. I mean, even I know better than that. But his gaze just kept coming back to me and I said to him, 'Lloyd, turn. There's a utility pole.' But he just said, 'yeah, uh-huh' and didn't listen and didn't look. I was too smitten to notice that he didn't have a lick of common sense."

"He was nice, though. Unlike a few of your boyfriends." Aubrey began cutting her steak.

It was interesting, sitting with a view of both sisters. They were identical but the more he got to know Ava, the more different the two of them looked. Similar, but different. Aubrey was more composed and sensible, clearly the more respon-sible of the two, always there to watch over Ava. The way she studied him, as if he'd met with her approval, made him think she wouldn't mind handing over the caretaking of Ava to him. Good to know. It was nice feeling to have her sister's positive opinion.

"I didn't date for a while," Ava continued. "Until I was out of high school."

"That's because I had my accident," Aubrey added, setting down her steak knife. "I jump horses, and one day in the middle of a competition, my mare went down. On top of me. She broke her leg and I cracked my hip and back. It took us both a long time to recover. Ava was there helping me faithfully without complaint."

"It was my privilege to be there with you," Ava said.

There was no mistaking the affection between the sisters as their gazes met.

"Then there was Brett," Aubrey began.

Ava pealed with laughter. "Oh, Brett. He was the worst. He was like a stalker. But did I figure that out right away? No. We'd dated two years and he'd proposed. That's when he went really strange."

"Plus, he was mean to you."

"Yeah, but I was going to cooking school and working full-time at the bookstore. That was before Dad and Dorrie retired to Arizona, so I had to help out at home, I never had a spare minute to just sit down and think. Or I *might* have noticed it. It started out subtle at first."

"He was sarcastic right up front." Aubrey corrected. "Then it snowballed from there, especially after the proposal."

"Exactly." Ava rolled her eyes, adorable and sweet and as wholesome as the sunshine glittering on the spray of the fountain, a bright sparkle that he would never tired of watching.

Show me the way, Lord. He felt the conviction deep in his soul. *Do I have a chance here?*

"Well, he would get sharp or distracted or gruff, but he'd be tired. He was going to school full-time, too. But it kept getting worse and there's no excuse for that. So I gave him his ring back, and then he started turning up wherever I went. Apparently, he thought I had another boyfriend on the side. Like I'd want another one. So it sounds like I've had boyfriend after disastrous boyfriend, but it hasn't been that many."

"Just that disastrous, but serious. Lloyd had proposed too," Aubrey commented. "This is why I don't date. Ava's experiences have scared me."

He watched the way the sisters laughed together, seeming amused and not traumatized by their experiences. "So you both have a no-man no-dating policy?"

"Well, mine is more habit," Aubrey said.

"Mine is a philosophy. I date guys that *seem* great."

"You have a talent for it—" Aubrey started.

"—But then when I really get to know them, it's not the truth," Ava finished. "They're marginally moral at best. Or so-so, or have secret habits like gambling. What's a girl to do? The Mr. Yucks look nice on the outside. It isn't until you get to know them that you see them for who they are, and see the things they are trying to keep hidden. It's that fault-blindness, not a good trait to have in the dating world."

Ava shrugged, and there it was, the hint of sadness at the corners of her eyes, dimming the wattage of her smile. There was a lot of pain there. More than she was going to talk about.

"I'm not like that," he said. "I don't run off, I don't leave, and I don't have destructive habits. Just so you know. I'm respectful toward women, I'm not mean and I try as hard as I can to be one of the good guys."

Ava sighed. Yeah, she was noticing that about him, and his words made her soul ache with longing. He could capture her heart, if she let him.

And wasn't that the problem? Brice Donovan could be her downfall. The one thing she could never do was amend her policy, because if she dated him and fell in love with him, he could hurt her most of all.

He was like a dream man and too good to be true.

A few hours later, the sun was sinking into the amethyst peaks of the Rockies as Ava guided the SUV out of Brice's winding subdivision. Talk about gorgeous homes. She tried to focus her thoughts on the road, on how Rex had hopped into the driver's seat of the SUV when they went to leave, wanting to go with her.

She tried *not* to think of the man who'd grabbed his stubborn dog by the collar, kindly helping him down. He was a dream man. So where did that leave her? In more trouble than she'd been when she'd agreed to dinner. Now what? How was she going to resist him now?

"He's a great cook." Aubrey yawned. "I haven't had that good a dinner since Gran was up from Arizona."

One more thing to add to the growing list of the great things about Brice Donovan. Ava negotiated a corner, slowed to a stop and checked for traffic on the main road. "I know where you're going with this."

"He likes you, you like him. Why won't you go out with him? I wouldn't be surprised if he's asked you out and you turned him down."

"I never said I liked him."

"You don't have to. Do you know what your problem is?"

Ava stared extra hard at the road. "I don't need you to tell me."

"Yes, you do. That's why God assigned me to you. I'm telling you this for your own good."

"Please don't." Ava pulled to a stop at another stop sign, staring in frustration at the city laid out like glitter in the twilight valley. "I know you mean well, but I've got things under control."

"You never have *anything* under control. You like Brice so much, you're afraid of it."

"Not that I'll admit."

"Ha! See? You're in the denial stage. Remember? Katherine was there after she met Jack, and she wouldn't admit it either, but she was."

"Denial is a very effective coping method. Except for the fact that I'm totally *not* in denial. I have a policy, remember? I'm dedicating my life to making the world a sweeter place. I'm on a mission. I will not be distracted by anything."

Even she could hear how those words were hollow—they were no longer the whole truth. No matter how hard she willed them to be, they fell short of what she now knew to be honest.

How had that happened? It was like sand shifting beneath the rock of her foundation and now she had to readjust everything.

Aubrey was only being caring, kind and gentle in that way of hers; and she was always right. Ava knew it, but she wasn't ready to admit this to herself. Because as long as she was in denial, then she wouldn't have to make a decision. She wouldn't have to acknowledge that caring about Brice was no longer her choice. Her heart was just doing it.

"Ava, do you know how great this guy is? He's wonderful. He really cares about you. He invited me to come along tonight, and none of the other guys you've dated ever welcomed me and included me the way Brice has. The way he looks at you and the way he talks to you, it says one thing. He likes you. He didn't care that you drained half his pool of water with all your cannonballs."

"Hey, you helped with that."

"Yes, but I don't make as big of a splash. I lack your finesse and skill."

"True."

They smiled together.

"And what about the beautiful woodwork he's doing for you? Ava, he's working over the weekend. I don't think he has to work overtime to keep his personal budget in the black."

"Probably not." Did she tell Aubrey that Brice had wanted to give her this dream? And that was really starting to affect her?

"Ava, he had worked up two different scrollwork patterns for you to choose from. That's a big deal."

"Not if I don't think about it."

They had reached the outskirts of town, and the traffic was light. She concentrated on driving, which was a lot easier than concentrating on how Brice had brought her two two-foot lengths of wood, carefully detailed, from his home workshop. One had rosebuds and leaves, and the other had cabbage roses. He'd made no big deal about it, but she knew it was more. That was scaring her, too.

Aubrey hit her second wind when they turned into their apartment complex. "Okay, I have one more thing to say, and then I'm done. You've finally found a good guy. A man of substance who sees how special you are. He's not like the others."

"You mean, after I get to know him I won't see that he's not right for me, before my heart is broken?"

"At least you see the pattern."

"It isn't just me. We've all had such a hard time getting attached, I mean, Katherine's in her thirties and she's finally getting married. Spence? Well, look at him, he drives every nice woman away before she can say 'hi.' Do you think it's because Mom left us like that? We already know love ends."

"*Some* love ends. Mom wasn't happy. Don't you remember?"

Remember? Painfully. *You make a mess of every-thing. You ruin everything. I can't take it anymore.* Her mother's last words to her. Haunting her after all these years.

Ava maneuvered into their reserved covered spot and cut the engine. She even remembered to take the keys out of the ignition.

Aubrey didn't move to unbuckle her seat belt. "Not all love ends. Look at Dad. He stayed. He never left. He loved us enough to stick it out, even when things were devastating for him. After Mom left, he was so lost and overwhelmed with respon-sibility. Remember?"

It had been a tough time for all of them. Dad trying to hold it together, lost doing housework and cooking. His sadness was suffocating and Ava had felt the responsibility for their mom's leaving. Although what Aubrey said *was* true. Dad had stayed. He'd never let them down.

It hurt too much to dwell on that, too. She climbed outside into the stifling heat, the chlorine scent of the water from Brice's pool clung to her skin and clothes, reminding her. Of him. Of what her heart wanted. That Aubrey was right.

That still didn't mean it was the smartest thing to disregard common sense and believe in one man—to put all her heart and soul, and all the love she had, on the line. For some reason she felt that seven-year-old girl inside her, feeling small and alone and wishing she could be different, so that *everything* could be different.

The sun was setting through bright magenta and orange clouds, casting a mauve light that glowed on the ordinary asphalt shingle rooftops and changed them to shining satin. Rose-pink glinted along the white siding of the two-storey buildings and reflected in windows.

The light cast over her too, and she felt hope lift though her like grace.

Chapter Ten

The bookstore's after-hours' quiet made her little sigh sound like a hundred-mile-per-hour gust of wind, which wasn't her intention. Now everyone was going to stop their inventory work and come hunt her down and ask, "What's wrong, Ava?"

She could hear the question already—mostly because it's what they always asked. She was the kind of girl who had one kind of problem after another, and her family was slightly enmeshed in her affairs.

She crept forward a few inches on her rug-burned knees, ignoring the rough rasp from the industrial carpet. Did she remember her knee pads? No. She'd forgotten for the past four nights in a row straight. She'd been on the run, from sun up and well into the dark of night, working, trying to figure out the malicious concept of bookkeeping—to no avail—and baking. Running errands. Picking up as many hours here at the bookstore as she could, which was why she was helping with inventory. She hated inventory, but the sad truth was, she needed the money. Big time.

She may have borrowed a chunk from Gran, but she'd only borrowed what was absolutely necessary for start-up, not for her wages or anything else. *A shoestring start-up,* that's what Gran called it and while she'd offered more of a loan, Ava had refused. She'd appreciate the funds, but she wasn't out to take advantage of her grandmother, whom she loved very much. So, she was on a shoestring. She would just work harder to make ends meet, that's all.

The problem was, she wasn't as efficient as she could have been, and why? Who was to blame?

Brice Donovan. Thoughts of him were distracting her in a big way. Not that she'd seen him since they'd had dinner at his house. She'd run out of any hopes of actually seeing him. For four straight workdays she'd been by the bakery early every morning to drop off goodies. And every evening, except for today, she'd checked the work after the construction dudes had left. She'd been excited by the renovation's progress, but there'd been no sight of Brice. Sure, he'd left messages on her cell. And she'd left messages on his. But did they actually speak? No.

She'd even received a chocolate cake order from

Brice's secretary for delivery to the office on Friday afternoon. Why hadn't he called with that? Or at least left a message? He'd given her the full court press with his charm and his cooking and now when she was considering softening her policy, was he available to hear it? No-oo.

Ava halted in mid-row and stared helplessly at the titles on the shelf and the clipboard on the floor beside her. Oops. Now she'd lost her place on the shelf, again. She stared down at the print out, and it started to blur. Probably because she'd been up since 4:45 a.m. that morning. It was now nearly nine—at night. She was totally beat.

"Ava?" Katherine rounded the corner of the history section, concern on her face. "What's wrong? You look exhausted. Why don't you take a break?"

Spence's voice sounded muffled coming from the other side of the row. "It's not time for her break. And she came in late. *Again.*"

Katherine planted her hands on her slender hips and shook her head. She looked calm and classic, as always, even casually dressed for their late night work session in a simple butter-yellow knit top and black boot-cut jeans.

How did Katherine do it? She carried as much of the responsibility of the bookstore as Spence did, but with such serene, easy grace. No sharp words of frustration, ever. She looked gorgeous and totally put together and never missed her Bible study groups, had started a weekly woman's reading group program and found time to date, fall in love with Jack, get engaged and teach the teenager to drive.

"I don't need a break," Ava confessed, feeling so totally like a frumpy failure right then. She knew her hair was falling out of the comb holder thingy for the billionth time. Aubrey had talked her into wearing it this morning. She stood up to stretch and noticed that her linen blouse had wrinkled so much, it looked as if she'd been sleeping in it. "I need junk food."

"Pizza?" asked the teenager—more commonly known as Hayden, Jack's kid. "Or how about French fries?"

"Nachos," Aubrey hollered from four stacks over. "With the works."

"No food near the books!" Spence sounded particularly annoyed. "And no breaks. I want this done before midnight."

Before midnight. Ava didn't want to think about how little sleep that meant she was going to get. But the good news was that she'd be able to make her next month's car payment.

"You look like a mess." Aubrey appeared and went straight to the comb clip thingy. "You didn't put this in right."

"I don't know how to put it in right." Ava rolled her eyes. "I'm so glad this is the last night we have to do this. Tomorrow night, I'm going to crash in front of the TV. The only time I plan on moving will be to answer the door for the pizza delivery guy. You too, Aubrey?"

"No. I have plans, I know you forgot. I'm going to that singles church function in the valley." Aubrey ran her fingers through Ava's hair and gathered it up in a neat coil. "And you were going to babysit for Danielle, so she can go on a date with her husband? Remember?" Even the thought of those fried tater tots made her feel perky.

"I'm too exhausted and hungry to remember anything. I think mexifries will help."

"There there's only one solution. We need junk food if we're going to last until midnight." Aubrey repositioned the Venus-flytrap-looking comb. "Spence, we're going to take another break."

"No breaks." He sounded angry, and there was a thud, like a few books tumbling from a shelf. He made an even angrier sound.

Aubrey took a step back to consider the comb's positioning. "He's extra crabby tonight."

"You distract him, and I'll slip out the back. Maybe he won't notice I'm gone."

"I'll notice," Spence barked, closer than they thought.

"Go." Katherine took Ava's clipboard. "I'll finish for you. Hayden, what do you want to order?"

"Uh…" The teenager poked her head around the corner. "I dunno."

"Hey, you come with me," Ava decided. "I'll

need help carrying all that food. Katherine, I'm going to need money."

"I *knew* you were going to say that. Help yourself to a couple of twenties from my purse. Our late-night snack will be my treat."

Super-duper. It might not be the answer to her frustration about Brice, but there was nothing like a fast-food fix, right? If you order enough fried food, you could forget a lot of problems. Distraction, that was the key to coping.

After finding cash in Katherine's purse, she grabbed her own. The first thing she checked was her cell, already knowing what she'd see. One missed call. A voice mail message.

She hit the button and waited to connect as she went in search of her keys.

"Are these them?" Hayden asked standing in front of the open refrigerator. There they were, on the shelf next to the soda cans.

"Hey, you're pretty useful for a teenager," Ava winked at the girl while she listened to her one message.

Brice's deep baritone was a welcome sound. "Tag, you're it. Try me back when you're off work at the bookstore. I'll be up late."

Okay, at least there was hope. She dialed his number, pushed open the back door and held it for the teenager. Hayden bopped through with coltish energy and waited while Ava made sure the door locked after them. She didn't want the backdoor burglar to try to rob the place. Poor Spence had enough pressure without that.

She got Brice's voice mail. Big surprise. "It's your turn to call me," she said and turned her ringer to the loudest setting. For added measure, so the phone didn't get muffled by all the junk in her bag, she slipped it into an outside pocket. There. She was all set. "Kid, do you still have my keys?"

"Yep. I was kinda hopin' that you'd let me drive. You know, cuz I gotta practice so I can ace my driver's test."

"Deal." She opened the passenger's side door and hopped onto the seat. She was pretty exhausted and look, she had a chauffeur. Cool. "When Katherine marries your dad, I won't mind too much that you're my new niece. I mean, I could probably endure it."

"Like I guess I could, too." Hayden looked happy as she took control behind the wheel. "So, what taco place is it? And how do I get there?"

"You have much to learn. Lucky for you, you have me to teach you. We always go to Mr. Paco's Tacos. They have the best nachos and mexifries. If you turn left out of the driveway, we can go past my shop on the way there. I want to see how the final coat of paint looks."

"You'll hire me when you open up, right?"

"Are you kidding? I thought you were going to work for free. I *could* pay you, I guess." Ava winked.

Hayden's smile was pure happiness. "You gotta teach me how to make monster muffins."

"In good time. Just drive, kid." Ava pulled out her phone just to check it.

No call. She knew that because she would have heard it ringing, but she had to check. Thinking of Brice at least made her feel a little closer to him when he felt so far away. Not that she wanted to admit it, but she missed him.

Big time.

In the quiet of Ava's shop, Brice swiped the sweat from his forehead and uncapped a bottle of water. He downed half of it in one swig. He was hot, tired and hungry. But he didn't want to break until he'd installed the last of the ceiling moldings. He'd have to bust his hump tomorrow, put in a long day, to get this finished before the cleaning crew pulled up tomorrow—Friday—afternoon.

The week had gone by in a blur, too fast, and without Ava. He'd heard about the morning baked goods that she'd provided faithfully every morning. He'd heard about the free certificates she'd handed out to all the workers this morning along with the colorfully decorated little coffee cakes. He'd been busy in his shop, finishing the last of the intricate scrollwork.

He missed her. He knew she was working late shifts at the bookstore—she'd left a message on his voice mail telling him about it. They had been playing phone tag all week. The lack of contact frustrated him, but he had to get this right for her. It was her dream, which was important to him. Important for her.

The soft yellow walls had warmed like sunshine during the day and now, with the honey glow of the varnished woodwork, the place was better than any picture. He couldn't wait for her to see it, but he wanted everything done first. He wanted it perfect for her.

Which meant only one thing. Time to get back to work. He recapped the bottle, set it on the sawhorse next to his cell and noticed a green light was flashing. A missed call.

No. He'd missed her again. He'd either been hammering or running the saw—he hadn't heard it ring. He snatched it up, ready to hit the speed dial, but before he could, he glanced up and there she was. She stood on the passenger side of her SUV, closing the door, looking through the windows directly at him. There was surprise on her face and disbelief in her eyes as she remained frozen in place.

He crossed to the door in three strides and threw the bolt. The night air was balmy as he moved toward her.

"Oh, I can't believe this. Brice, this is wonderful. What are you doing here, working so late?"

His heart rolled over. She looked so dreamy, so precious. It was hard to believe that she was real and that he hadn't imagined her here.

"I didn't expect you to show up here like this." He studied her dear face. She looked tired, but happy. That's why he'd worked long endless hours in his shop. He wanted her to be happy. With the woodwork. With the shop. With him. "It was supposed to be a surprise for you. I wanted it finished before you came by in the early morning."

"But—" Her fingers caught tightly around his. "It's nine-thirty at night and you're still working. Were you going to work all night?"

"However long it takes."

"But that's so much work."

"It's my pleasure, Ava."

"But—" Her lovely eyes shone, as if she understood, finally. "This is my dream. It's like you could look right into my heart and know."

"Amazing, don't you think?"

Ava was starting to believe it. She could feel it in the marrow of her bones. Aubrey was right, okay, she was *always* right. *What about the beautiful woodwork he's doing for you? I don't think he has to work overtime to keep his personal budget in the black.*

This had to be so much work. This was such a big deal. This was more than business. More than friendship. This was everything that totally scared her.

"Want to go inside and see?" His hand was so strong as he guided her toward the door. He felt as invincible as titanium, like a man a woman could believe in.

She'd been fooled before, but those times faded like shadows to light. Looking at him—being with him—filled her with true hope. He awakened a part of her that had been never been wholly alive before—an optimistic part of her spirit. That positive force seemed to fill her senses, overwhelming all common sense, so that she couldn't think of anything else but Brice, standing so tall and good.

It would be easy to lose perspective. She had to move slow, be smart, think things through and not rush into anything too fast. "Let's go inside so I can see everything a little better."

"Sure." His hand moved to the middle of her back, guiding her.

She turned at the door and gestured to the teenager still behind the wheel. "Like I'm going to leave you out here? C'mon."

"Who are you talking to?" he asked.

"My personal chauffeur. Brice, meet Hayden Munroe, my future niece, she's driving tonight."

"Good to meet you," Brice said politely, but Hayden only stared at him in shock. "Munroe. Your dad wouldn't be Jack Munroe, would he?"

"Yep. He's a state trooper. Did he like pull you over and give you a speeding ticket?"

"No. I'm a faithful follower of all traffic laws. But I met him at a charity golf match last month. To benefit the children's hospital wing. He beat the socks off me."

"That's my Dad." Hayden gave a shy smile and stepped through the open door.

Ava followed her, taking in the full effect of Brice's work. Their footsteps echoed in the tall ceilings painted the faintest shade of yellow, so that they looked white as they angled upwards. There were gaping holes where the tract lighting was supposed to fit, but the ceiling moldings were already mounted around half of the room, separating the airiness of the ceiling from the warm buttery walls.

How many hours had all of this taken him? Ava could only stare in disbelief. The careful rosebud design was everywhere—not overdone, not ornate, but subtle and whimsical. Like something out of a country painting come to life.

His hand came to rest on her shoulder, a light touch, and a claiming one. She could feel the weight of it and his heart's question.

"What do you think?" His baritone rumbled dangerously close to her ear.

Dangerous because any amount of proximity was too close for her comfort. Panic beat with frantic, sharp edges against her ribs, but she held her ground. She stayed near to him instead of bolting away. "It's unbelievable. You must have worked so hard."

"True. And?"

"You know I love it." He'd done all this work, taken an infinite amount of care, done all of this. For her. How was she going to resist him now? She looked at the lovely work, the careful beveling, the meticulous detail, the perfection that glowed like varnished sunshine. "Thank you."

"You're welcome." His fingers curled into her shoulder, not bruising, not harsh, but tender. "You know what this means, don't you?"

A more-than-friends policy. "That's everything I'm afraid of."

"I know, but you don't need to be."

She could totally fall in love with Brice. Head over heels, the whole shebang. She was already halfway there.

"Hey, this is so cool," Hayden said from the corner where she was tracing some of the lovely scrollwork with her fingertips. "There's a heart inside some of these roses. Do you have to like carve this or something?"

"Or something," he answered the teenager, but he didn't take his eyes from Ava, who went to the kid's side for a closer look.

Ava was endearing. Her golden hair was pulled back at the crown of her head to bounce in a curling fall down the graceful column of her neck. Her gauzy top could have been something a fairy tale princess might wear, and her modest denim shorts and rubber flip flops made her seem even more wholesome and sweet. She traced the intricate scrollwork with her forefinger. Tears filled her eyes and did not fall. She stood still, studying the work, framed by the pale yellow walls and the dark rectangles of uncovered windows.

His heart filled with devotion for her. Afraid to scare her more with the seriousness of his affection, he waited, letting her have the time she needed to see what he'd done for her.

"This is amazing, Brice." Her smile was a little wobbly. "I love it."

She didn't say more. She didn't need to. The moment their gazes met, he could feel a rare, inexplicable connection forge between them. An emotional bond that was already so strong, what would it become if given more time?

He thought he knew the answer to that, too.

"I'm glad you like it," he said.

The niece-to-be wandered around, appraising. "I thought this was like supposed to be done tomorrow."

"We will be," he answered her but could not look away from Ava. From her violet-blue eyes silvered with tears and her heart showing.

He brushed at her tears with the pads of his thumbs, feeling like he was ready for this.

He dropped a kiss on the tip of her nose. "Rex will be sad he missed you. He has a strict ten o'clock bedtime or he's grumpy the next day."

"I'll make an extra treat for him tomorrow. Will you be here?"

"To do the final walk-through with you. How does four o'clock sound? Will it work with your schedule?"

"I have no idea. Let me check." She pulled open

the top of her enormous shoulder bag and began pawing through it. "No, no, no. Oh, here it is." She filed through a small appointment book and found the correct date. "It looks like I can make it at four. Will it take very long?"

"Not at all," he said. "I've got plans at five."

"Perfect." She ought to be done in plenty of time to babysit for Danielle. "This means that our business will be concluded. Done. Over."

"That's right." He flashed her that drop-dead gorgeous killer grin of his, full wattage, and showed both sets of dimples. "I guess it's time to work on amending our friends-only policy. I'll see you at four?"

"Four." Ava blinked, but that didn't help. Her mind had gone completely fuzzy. It was as if all her gray matter had turned into one big cotton ball. "If I could say thank you for the next decade without stopping, it wouldn't feel like enough."

"It's enough." He took a step back and held open the door. "Why are you two out and about this late?"

"The kid and I are on a fast-food run. It's our last night of inventory and we desperately need nachos to keep going."

"Let me guess. Mr. Paco's Tacos. One of my favorite places."

"Really? And here I thought after visiting your posh house and snazzy pool, that you ate only gourmet. Little did I know we share a love of Mr. Paco's nachos."

"The burritos, too."

"Don't even go there. My stomach is going to start growling and that would be so embarrassing." *Embarrassing*. That word hit her like a punch. She was gaping up at him like she was totally love-struck. How embarrassing was that? As if she'd let herself fall in love with him so fast. Not!

She was in total control of her emotions.

A distant ring penetrated her thoughts and broke the moment between them. Ava stepped back, fished through her bag again and came up with her cell. She saw the bookstore's number on her screen and she groaned. "It's Spence. I'm not going to answer this."

"Spence. He's a little wound up," Hayden said. She'd stationed herself by the door. "I don't like it when he's so mad. We better go."

"Yeah, or we'll be punished with that disap-pointed look of his." She dumped her phone back into her bag. Eventually it would stop ringing, but she had bigger concerns right now—and he was standing directly in front of her. Brice. "Should we come back with nachos for you? Or a burrito?"

"No, I'm good. Thanks."

"Okay." She took a step closer to the door, but she didn't want to say goodbye. She told herself it was the beautiful woodwork she couldn't tear herself away from. That wasn't the truth, but it was easier than admitting the truth.

She didn't want to leave Brice, because she knew

she'd miss him. And in caring for him so much, she was terrified. "Good night," she said, as if she were in complete control of her heart, went up on tiptoe to brush a chaste kiss to his cheek and walked out of the shop. But when she'd settled in the passenger's side of her SUV, she realized she'd left something behind.

Her heart.

Chapter Eleven

Another drive-by baking. Brice had arrived just in time to see the back of a yellow vehicle far down the street, too far away for her to notice him. Rex seemed disappointed, too. He'd dashed to the kitchen only to find the box and a note on a star-shaped, bright-yellow Post-it note.

> Sorry, I promised the teenager monster muffins for her church thing today, so I'm running short on time. I've left gifts for the dudes and their families. And a special treat for my true love, Rex.

He wasn't surprised by her curlicue script or the fact that the note was written in glittery pink ink. There were a dozen medium-sized gift boxes set behind the regular baking box. One had his name on it, so he snooped beneath the lid. A small individually decorated cake and a gift certificate.

Rex whined with impatience, his tail thumping.

"You have one here, too." Curious, Brice peeked into the box with Rex's name written in glittery gold ink. It was full of large, bone-shaped snacks.

Ava *would* have a recipe for fancy dog treats. He tossed one to Rex, who caught it in mid-air and gobbled it in two bites. It had to be delicious because his eyes brightened and he sat perfectly, the very best behavior ever witnessed. This dog obviously wanted another one.

Okay, he was a sucker. Brice tossed him one more before he went straight to work. He had a few touch-ups to do and the display case glass to pick up.

He was totally beat. He'd put in a hard week's work, but it was worth it. At exactly four-thirty this afternoon, their final walk-through would be complete and their business deal over. Then their relationship could get personal.

And he'd planned in a big way. He had reservations. A jet. A limo. Everything all lined up. By the time the jet touched back down at the local private airport tonight around ten-thirty, he hoped that Ava would have a better idea just what she meant to him. What he wanted to mean to her.

This might be the hardest thing he'd ever done. To lay his heart on the line. But what choice did he have? He loved her. No holds barred. No going back. All the way until forever—if that's what she wanted.

The hard thing about falling in love was that it took two to get to there. Ava had to make a decision now. He knew she was afraid, she'd been hurt. It was hard for her to risk again. He knew how she felt. He was scared, too.

With God's help, maybe they could take that risk together.

The late afternoon sun was in Ava's eyes as she screeched to a stop in front of the bakery. Wow, no one was around, just one green pickup parked in the shade. The brand new windows were so clean they shone, and gave a perfect view into the cozy little shop space.

It was perfect, and her heart gave a little twist. She'd never dared dream as much as this. Even from the outside, the pale yellow walls warmed with the direct sunshine and seemed to invite a person right in. The empty display case sparkled, too, and the honey-colored wood was a comforting, homey touch.

Best of all, there was Brice, standing with his boots planted, wearing a knit black shirt and trousers, looking like a hundred on a scale of ten. There was no mistaking the intensity of his look or the reason why she felt joy light up in her heart.

It was his joy. His light.

Time to work on amending our friends-only policy, so think about the terms for our next agreement. His words had been troubling her since they'd talked last night.

So had Hayden's. Once they'd driven away,

she'd said so innocently. "Wow, is that your boy-friend? Isn't he like rich and really cool?"

Yeah, so why was he interested in me? That was another insecurity that had plagued her every second, all day long. But seeing him coming toward her with his powerful athletic stride, knowing the gladness on his face was from seeing her made those insecurities whisper a little more quietly.

She grabbed her bag, tossed her phone inside and hopped out of the car. The door slammed shut before she realized her hand was empty—no keys. But the locks didn't automatically set, so she could open the door right back up and grab the keys from the ignition—thanks to Brice.

"You are so handy to have around, I can't believe it," she smiled at him.

"Good to know." The look he gave showed her he was glad to see her.

Somehow she had to *stop* liking him more every time she saw him. Otherwise, she was going to be a total goner. She'd fall all the way in love before the evening was over.

"I dropped the check for the last half of the payment at the office on my way here. Along with a dozen monster muffins."

"I bet the office staff was happy. That was nice of you. You must be awfully pleased with the work. Everybody waits until after the walk-through and the punch list is finished before they hand over that much money."

"It just felt strange to give you a check, so I left it with your bookkeeper."

"Because you're past the business-only phase, too?" he asked.

Okay, she could officially admit it. "Just a little bit. Maybe."

"Me, too. Just a little bit. *Maybe*." But when he said it, the words sounded as if he didn't have a doubt in the world. He took her hand, twining his big strong fingers between hers, holding on to her as if she mattered, as if she had so much value to him.

For now, that pesky little voice whispered inside her. That'll change. Just give him time.

It took all her inner might to silence that voice. To accept the cherished feeling of having him at her side, of his hand to hers, palm to palm.

"Let's get this over with because I have plans for you." His fingers tightened on hers, strengthening their connection. "Are you ready?"

"As ready as I'll ever be."

He held the door for her, a gentleman all the way. She tried to keep her emotions in check, but the sunshine spilling over her made her feel more than hopeful. Made her intensely aware of her blessings.

What if this was a sign that her luck in life was changing? This charming shop with wood-wrapped windows, cathedral ceilings and whimsical warmth had once existed only in her dreams.

Now it was real.

Maybe it was time to see if more of her dreams in life could come true.

"Four twenty-nine." Brice checked his watch and glanced over the top of Ava's head. No sign of the limo yet, but the driver still had another minute. "I'm glad you're happy with our work."

"Happy doesn't begin to describe it. I still can't believe this was so painless. And the work your men did here. I'm grateful to all of you."

He could see that this transition from friends-only to more than friends was hard for her, too. She was nervously glancing toward the front door. Trying to escape before he hit the serious questions? he wondered. Or being afraid that he didn't have any?

This was tough for him, too. He'd never been this nervous. He'd never felt as if he had so much on the line. Everything was riding on this—his heart, his hopes and his future. It was tough letting go and trusting God's will for him. Brice took a shaky breath, gathering his courage. He'd have to see how this worked out. It wasn't easy not knowing.

"There's the limo now." He set the clipboard aside to cradle her chin in his hands. "Remember I said I had plans for you?"

"Y-yes. I vaguely recall something to that effect."

"And that we needed to renegotiate our friends-only policies?"

"Yes, but why the limo?" Panic coiled through her.

He could feel her fear. "It's okay. I have plans. Nice plans, involving dinner and watching the sun set. It should be painless, maybe even romantic. Are you interested?"

"Tonight? I c-can't."

His heart took a blow. He'd really thought she felt this, too. He took a step back and released his hold on her. "Well, I had to ask."

"Wait—no, I'm not saying 'no.'" She looked tortured. "When you said you had plans, I was thinking more of that next step. You know, like you'd ask me out sometime soon. I didn't know that you meant tonight. Now you're mad."

"I'm not mad."

"I told Danielle that I'd babysit for her. Aubrey has this church thing, and everyone else is busy. Spence could do it, but we don't want him to scare the children. So there's nobody else but me. You're looking madder."

"No. I just…made…plans."

See? Already she was messing this up. How did she do it? And so fast. They'd been officially more than friends for two minutes, maybe three? She twisted around to get a good look at the limo. It was shiny white and one of the long ones with sparkling windows and it looked expensive. "What kind of plans did you make?"

"Nothing that can't be rearranged for another time."

There it was, the terrible sense of foreboding,

that everything so wonderfully right in her life was about to go totally wrong. Doom would strike and then it would all be over. She would never know what it would be like to be cherished by this man.

"I'll be back." Brice strode away, shoulders set, spine straight, purposefully.

Oh, no. Every last one of her hopes plummeted. What plans had she messed up? She closed her eyes, took a deep breath and tried to get centered enough to pray. But she couldn't. She was all messed up inside, as if someone had taken a big stick to her vat of negative feelings and was stirring it hard.

The door opened with a faint swoosh. Brice's powerful, wonderful presence filled the room.

"C'mon," he said in his kind voice, the one that made all the fears inside her melt like butter on a hot stove. His hand settled on her nape, and his touch, his kindness, seared through her like hope. He opened the door.

"Okay, call me confused." She stared at the driver in his suit and cap, holding open the passenger door for her. "What about Danielle?"

"Rick is going to take you to Danielle's house. I'm going to borrow your SUV and swing through and pick up take out so we all have something to eat. I'm coming with you tonight instead. My plans can change. Yours shouldn't."

"You mean…you're going to babysit with me?"

"Do you have a problem with that?"

She was vaguely aware her jaw was hanging open, but she couldn't seem to make it shut. She couldn't seem to move anything at all. All she could do was stare at this man—this perfect man—and feel even worse. How was she going to keep from falling one hundred percent in love with him *now?*

Brice held out his hand. "Your keys?"

She went in search and found them in her pocket. Did he know what this meant to her?

"I'll see you soon." He leaned close, so close she could smell the faint scent of fabric softener on his shirt.

Her spirit lifted from simply having him near.

He pressed a sweet kiss to her cheek. "I know family is important to you. That means, since we're dating, your family is important to me."

She sank onto the leather seat, dazed. This wasn't a dream, was it?

Brice knelt down on the sidewalk until they were eye to eye. "We are dating, right?"

"Right." Her entire soul smiled.

"All right," Danielle said, dragging Ava into the kitchen. "When did you start dating Brice Donovan?"

"Officially about twenty minutes ago." Ava leaned over the counter to get a good look out the kitchen window. There he was, as gorgeous as a wish come true. He'd climbed out of her SUV and was now carting with him a box of drinks and several big food bags bearing the Mr. Paco's Tacos emblem.

"Why didn't I know about this? You girls aren't supposed to leave me out of the loop!" Danielle looked rushed as she grabbed her purse and rummaged around for something. She pulled out her cell and hit the power button. "You have my number, call if there's a problem. I just can't believe this. Brice Donovan. He's *wonderful*. Jonas knows him from the community of united churches charities board. They served on it together for a few years. He just raved about him. Oh, look, he's here. And I've got to go. I'm completely late."

"Don't worry. Tell that great husband of yours that it's all my fault. I was late in the first place."

"He expects it." With a wink, Danielle rushed to the door. "Madison's not to have sugar. Tyler will try to talk you into too much television."

"I know the scoop. Go. Before your husband holds it against me. It's okay that he's here, right?"

"Uh, yeah." Danielle grabbed her keys and rushed into the living room. After a final kiss to her little ones she headed to the garage door.

It closed the same moment there was a knock on the front door. She swung it open and wasn't prepared for how good it was to find him there. He could be anywhere tonight, but he'd chosen to be with her. Which worked out just fine since she wanted to be with him.

She took the drink box. "Come on in. The kids are watching TV. I like your choice of take out."

"I figured we couldn't go wrong with tacos." He shouldered past her. "Do you want this on the table?"

"Yep. I'll round up the munchkins."

Brice set the bags of food on the table and glanced around. He wasn't surprised by the comfortable-looking furniture and pictures of cute kids on the wall. Several family vacation photos were framed in recognizable places like the Grand Tetons and Yellowstone. It felt like a real home. Cheerful checks and ruffles sparingly decorated the kitchen and what he could see of the living room. There was a TV in a cabinet tuned to a wholesome-looking cartoon. A couch faced it.

Ava knelt down to talk to the kids out of his view on the couch. She was pure tenderness, and his heart thudded to the floor. She was truly a kind woman. No doubt about it, she'd make a great mom. It was a side of her he hadn't seen but guessed was there.

A preschool-aged boy hopped up, stood on the cushions and threw his arms around Ava. The kid wore a plastic fireman's hat and the brim bonked her in the temple when he gave her a wet smacking kiss, which she pretended was gross just to have him laughing. Then she tickled his stomach, reminded him of the rule about the couch and standing and watched while he jumped down with a two-footed thud.

"Did ya bring lotza mexifries?" he asked as he charged Brice's way. "Aunt Ava says I gotta have lotza mexifries or I'll get shorter insteada taller."

Yeah, he could see Ava telling that to the little guy. Funny. "Don't sweat it. I got the largest tub of them."

"Whew." As if that had been a big worry, the kid pulled back his chair, climbed up and settled into his booster seat.

Brice wasn't around kids very much, but this one was cute. He started unpacking the food. "You like tacos, kid?"

"Lots." The preschooler rested his elbows on the edge of the table and propped his chin on his hands. "Are you a fireman?"

"No. Are you?"

"Yep. I put out lotza fires today."

"Good work." Brice pulled the boxed kiddy meal from the giant bag.

He felt more than heard Ava's approach. It was as if his spirit turned toward her, recognizing her and only her. She had a curly-haired little girl on her hip, and the sight did something to him. She had the little girl laughing, her chubby cheeks pink with delight.

"Aunt Ava! Aunt Ava!" The boy shouted, holding up three sticky-looking fingers. "I put out three fires today."

"Sorry, I can't hear you," she teased as she slid the little girl into a high chair. "I'm deaf from you yelling so loud."

"Oops. My bad."

Brice didn't need to wonder where the kid had learned that—his gaze landed on Ava again as she double-checked the little girl's lap belt on the high chair, and satisfied, straightened. "Brice, I hope you brought a lot of mexifries. We don't want anyone at this table to get any shorter than they already are."

"I brought the biggest tub."

"My hero. It's hard for a girl not to like a guy who knows what's important in life."

"Mexifries are one of the real secrets to true happiness."

"Exactly." She peered into one of the food bags. "Nachos. Burritos. Tacos. I'm speechless with gratitude."

"Not hunger?"

"That, too. Let me get milk for the kids. If you want to start doling out the food?"

"Sure." As he got to work, the little tot across the table stared at him like she wasn't too sure she approved of his presence.

"Aunt Ava! Aunt Ava!" The boy twisted around on his knees and hung over the back of his chair. "I getta say grace! I getta say grace!"

"Okay, okay. But what's your mom's rule?" Ava asked from behind the refrigerator door.

"Umm." The kid appeared to be thinking extremely hard.

This was not his experience of a family, Brice thought as he put the tubs of mexifries in the middle of the table. His mom would have a coronary at the noise level. No laughing at the table. No yelling.

Sitting like a little gentleman—always. Use our best manners all the time.

All that had its place, but this was better. Comfortable. Fun. That was one of the things he cherished about Ava so much. She could make the simple things in life, like settling down to the dining room table, feel like a refreshing and cheerful kind of heaven on earth.

Ava slid a plate and a cup of milk in front of the boy. "No hats at the table, Tyler."

"Oh, yeah. I forgot." He handed her the bright red fireman's hat. "Can I say the blessing now?"

Ava dropped the hat on the back of the couch and returned to hand out another plate. "Brice, do you mind if Tyler does the honors?"

He could tell by the twinkling humor in her eyes that the boy's blessing was cute. Call him curious. He took the offered plate. "Sure."

"*Now*, Aunt Ava?"

"Hold on a minute." Ava rolled her eyes as she slid a cup on the toddler's tray.

"*Now?*" The kid sounded as if he were about to spontaneously combust.

"Now." Ava dropped into her chair.

Before Brice had time to bow his head, the little boy started in. "*Thanks for the eats, Lord. God bless us every one!*"

"Dickens' *A Christmas Carol* has made an impression on him," Ava explained after they'd muttered a quick "Amen." "He keeps watching this wholesome cartoon version of the movie over and over and it's driving Danielle insane."

Before Brice could answer, the boy hollered. "Aunt Ava! Hurry, I need mexifries. I'm shrinking."

"We can't have that. Brice, you look a little shorter, too."

He held out his plate. "Load me up."

What else could he say? This was exactly what he expected of an evening spent with Ava. Maybe not what he'd planned, but that didn't matter. All that mattered to him was being with her. For now and, he suspected, for his lifetime to come.

"I can't believe you're still talking to me," Ava said in the quiet of the warm night standing beside her SUV. It was dark out. Almost eleven o'clock. "Especially after Tyler squirted you with the hose."

"We were playing fireman, and it was an accident. I dried out pretty fast."

"You handled being drenched from head to toe in your snazzy clothes pretty well. Most men would have gotten really angry."

"I'm not like most men."

"I'm noticing that." It was hard not to.

Don't think about how perfect he is, she warned herself. That would just start making her nervous. Look at him, Mr. Fantastic, nice, wealthy and kind. He liked fast-food mexifries and went to church faithfully every Sunday. They'd talked about that after the kids had been in bed.

And after discussing faith, they went on to talk more about his family and hers. Chloe was still honeymooning in Fiji. His mom was ready to drive him nuts now that his sister was married off and she kept making elaborate plans for his upcoming birthday, and his dad was holding open a position at his investment firm, which Brice still didn't want.

She told of Katherine's upcoming wedding and all the planning that took, that she still hadn't picked a cake yet. She talked about their cousin Kelly who'd gotten married and was living in California on base with her marine husband. Then she mentioned the stress of owing her grandmother so much money.

Somehow they'd managed to avoid the more personal side of their conversation. Like, did he want kids? How many? She wanted children, but she had to find someone to get married to first. And wasn't that practically impossible? Certainly not a topic for a first date. If seeing her taking care of kids hadn't totally scared him off, talking about marriage and wanting kids would.

Then again, why risk it?

She dug through her purse for her keys. "It looks like you need a ride home."

"Nope, Rick should be arriving here in the next few minutes."

"Well, I don't want to leave you standing here alone."

"It's late. You've got to be tired from running after the kids. Go home." He smiled his billion mega-watt smile with the double dimples. "I'll be fine. I want you to drive safely."

"That's always my plan. I might not be the best driver, but I've never hit anything. Except for Grandpop's St. Bernard. I didn't see him in the rearview mirror."

Brice burst out laughing. "Does anything normal ever happen to you, or it is always a circus with you?"

"Always a circus. You've changed your mind about dating me. By the way, I didn't hurt Tiny at all."

"Tiny?"

"The St. Bernard. Not even a bruise. He didn't want us to leave and I couldn't see that he'd planted himself behind the car to stop us from going. He must have been in a blind spot because I checked the mirrors before I started backing up. There was this horrible thud. You should have seen the damage to Dad's bumper, though. It was the family car, and because they didn't want the insurance premium to go up, he didn't get it fixed. My family never let me live it down."

"And Tiny?"

"He learned to keep away from me when I was behind the wheel. I miss that guy. He passed away a month after Grandpop did." The pain of the loss still stole her breath. "Your grandparents are alive and well?"

"Thriving. They're vacationing at their home in Italy. They like to travel. They should be back for my birthday this week."

"I'm glad they are enjoying their lives. My grandparents always meant to do that, but they never got to travel much before they ran out of time to do it together."

"Our grandfathers were very close friends. I know he still advises your grandmother on her investments. Is she still living in Arizona?"

"She's stayed away since Grandpop passed. She said the house had too many memories of him, so she moved to their home in Scottsdale. They'd only had it for a few years, so I guess there weren't as many memories there. I think it helps her to be away, although we miss her. Dad's down there now, too, with Dorrie. They're all coming back at the end of summer for Katherine's wedding."

"My grandparents can't seem to breathe without the other. Were yours like that, too?"

"Gran said that losing her husband was like having her heart cut out. She's never been the same. They were very much in love. The real way."

"The way it's meant to be. My parents never managed to find that with each other." He shrugged. "They get along all right, they're compatible, but it's not what my grandparents have. They're tight."

"I know what you mean. Gran has always said Grandpop was her gift straight from heaven. She had all the best blessings in him." Okay, this was getting dangerously close to the topic she wanted to avoid, because she did not want to mess this up with Brice.

And yet, she couldn't seem to stop herself. "I've always thought they were the happily-ever-part of the fairy tale. You know, after Cinderella gets her shoe back *and* her prince, and Snow White is awakened by her prince, they end the stories. But I knew that kind of love was real because my grandparents lived for each other. They breathed together. It's what I always wanted."

Great going, Ava. She held her breath, *waiting,* just waiting, for him to start moving away.

But he didn't. "Me, too."

Headlights broke around the corner at that moment. It was Rick with his fancy limo and he pulled right up to the sidewalk, so Ava didn't know what else Brice had been about to say.

He brushed a kiss to her cheek. "Good night, beautiful."

Her soul sighed. "Wow, aren't you Mr. Perfect?"

"Oh, so it's working. Good to know I'm charming you."

"Only a tad. A smidgeon. A pinch."

Okay, that was an understatement. If she could measure how much Brice Donovan had impressed her, it would be the distance from the earth to the moon and back six hundred times.

Then he was gone, leaving her there in the light of the moon, unable to stop the full-blown wishes rising up from her soul.

Chapter Twelve

With hopeful cheer mid-afternoon light tumbled through the new larger front windows of her shop. But was she feeling hopeful? No. Astonished would be one word. Overwhelmed would be another.

She couldn't stop staring at the two dozen yellow, red-tipped roses Brice had sent. What was a girl to do when her hopes were already sky high, tugging like a helium balloon against the string? With every breath she took, she drew in the delicate fragrance of the lovely bouquet and tried to convince herself she wasn't scared.

The door behind her whispered open and there was Aubrey hefting a really big box. Ava caught the door, holding it as her twin tumbled inside.

"Whew, it's a scorcher out there. The air conditioning feels nice." Aubrey slid the box to the ground. "Those flowers are gorgeous. From Brice?"

It wasn't exactly a question. And it wasn't exactly what Aubrey was asking. Ava could feel their shared brain cells firing. Her sister knew how she felt. She knew what those roses meant.

It was a shocker how calm her voice actually sounded. "Yes, they just arrived. Isn't it a totally nice gesture?"

"Nice, sure. But a bunch of daisies is nice. Roses say something much more. Like the *L* word."

"The *L* word is none of your business, nosy." No sense in getting into a blind panic. "Brice and me, we're in that awkward more-than-friends stage, but not totally committed stage. Who knows how it's going to work out? Doom might be lurking out there somewhere, just waiting."

She had to be prepared for it, if it was.

"What doom? There's no doom." Aubrey went straight to the roses and inhaled deeply. "A man doesn't send something like this unless he's trying to sweep you off your feet."

"Yes, well, it's working."

"So, you called him to thank him, right? What did he say? Is he taking you out soon?" Aubrey pulled a pint carton of strawberry milk out of the box, still cold from the grocery store. She opened the spout and held it out for Ava to take. "What? You're just standing there not saying anything. You've called him, right?"

She took the milk. "Uh, I haven't got there yet."

"And you're procrastinating because…?"

"Okay, I can admit it. I'm a big chicken. Babysitting with him at Danielle's went so great. I mean, he was really Mr. Perfect. What if I mess this up?"

"Ava, Ava, Ava." Aubrey was using her gentlest voice, the one that was filled with so much unconditional sisterly love. It just proved that Aubrey was blinded by flaws, too. "This romance with Brice is totally new for you. You've finally found yourself a perfect guy."

"And it's too good to be true, right? That's what I'm afraid of." And much, much more, but could she admit that to Aubrey?

No.

"You are perfectly lovable. Mom was wrong to say that to you when she left. To blame you for her unhappiness. It wasn't true then."

"We're talking about men, not Mom."

"Okay." Aubrey's heart was showing. "Don't you think the crazy accusations would have scared him off if he was going to be?"

"I can't believe he helped me babysit. He said *my family is important to me, so it's important to him.*"

"See? How many signs do you need?"

"I don't know if there could be enough."

Aubrey traced the pattern of the tiny intricate roses carved into the trim of the gleaming, perfect case. "I really think his heart is true. I think he's the right man for you. Why don't you grab hold of this blessing the Lord is placing before you? Brice might be the happily-ever-after I've been praying for, for you. Just believe that God is in charge and embrace this chance."

"I'm scared I'm going to mess this up. That he's going to get a good look at me and see that I don't fit into the right image. That's what Brice is looking for. He wants someone from the same background and compatible lifestyle. Look at me, I'm not exactly mink-wearing, symphony-going material. You heard him talk about his fiancée."

"His ex-fiancée. Didn't you listen to him at all?"

"It's hard to hear really well with all this panic racing around inside my head."

"You're a nut." Aubrey rolled her eyes. "What am I going to do with you?"

"Not much. You're stuck with me."

"That's just my good luck." Aubrey smiled. "Call him. Take a deep breath and do it. Take the next step forward."

"Sure, what do I have to lose? It's only my heart at stake."

"Do you know what I think?" Aubrey knelt and began unpacking the box. "I think you're *more* scared this is going to work out."

"Uh, yeah."

"Go in the kitchen and call him. I'll watch the front. Oh, and I'll put up all this stuff I brought."

"Okey dokey. You're wonderful, you know that?"

"I do. Now go."

"Thanks, Aub."

Her cell was ringing as she streaked into the kitchen. Her heart jumped with jubilation when she saw Brice's name and number on her screen. Talk about perfect timing. Okay, she was scared, but this *had* to be a sign. She hit the talk button. "I love the flowers. Thank you."

"I know red roses are expected, but when I saw these in the florist's case, I thought of you. Bright yellow like the sunshine you are."

If he kept talking like that, he was going to scare her even more.

"What are you up to this morning?" he asked.

"No good, as usual. I just finished making a ballet shoe cake, it's for one of the construction dude's daughters."

"That was really nice of you, including certificates for a free birthday cake for everyone."

"It's the least I could do. My new kitchen is wonderful to work in. The question is, have you recovered from the trauma of babysitting?"

"No trauma to recover from. I'm made of tougher stuff than that. Remember how I said I had plans in place that we postponed?"

"You know I do." She heard a slight tinkle of chimes and peered through the open doorway. There was Aubrey hanging a beautiful ceramic bell over the door.

"I've been able to push those plans back a few weeks. I wanted to give you plenty of notice this time. I thought we could combine it with celebrations for the Fourth of July. You wouldn't be interested in spending that weekend with me would you?"

"Uh, did I hear you right? The entire weekend?"

"Now, before you start jumping to conclusions and questioning my morals, let me explain."

He was laughing, remembering their unforgettable first meeting when she'd told him to get some morals. At least he thought it was funny. That was a good sign, right?

"Okay, I'll wait for the explanation before I start firing insults."

"I have some property near Glacier National Park, and we won't be alone. I plan to invite my sister and her husband. My grandparents will be there, too. I was going to suggest that you invite Aubrey. We'll have a big cookout and watch fireworks over the lake. It'll be fun—and well chaperoned. What do you think?"

"Do you mean like going camping, or something? Because I try not to go too far out into the wilderness."

"Why? You're not a backcountry kind of girl?"

"If I tell you, then you'll stop dating me. Years from now you'll tell your friends it was a good thing you dumped me when you did."

"Not a chance, gorgeous."

She was in big trouble because her high hopes were rising higher than the galaxy. She was in bigger trouble because the logical part of her was drowned out by those rising hopes.

"Tell me about this story of yours, Ava. I gotta know."

"My dad loved to camp and he'd haul us all up to one of the national forests and we'd do the tent thing and the catch trout for supper thing and cook over an open campfire thing."

"Uh oh. I'm starting to see what might have been the problem here."

"I accidentally started a forest fire. It wasn't my fault. And it was only a little grass fire, but I never lived it down. Over the years the story has grown to gargantuan proportion and when Dad tells it now, you'd think I burned down half the western forests in the United States."

"And you started it how?"

"My marshmallow caught on fire. I was seven. I was afraid of flame, mostly, so I was sitting farther back than everyone else from the campfire. And Aubrey leaned over to say something to me and I forgot to watch the stick. It was sort of top heavy because I was holding the very end of it and it just sort of dipped into the fire.

"When I noticed that my marshmallow was turning black and spewing flame, I screamed and gave it a big shake. Blazing marshmallow fluff flew off the stick and onto Mom and Dad's tent. It caught fire, of course. It was a total disaster. Luckily, Dad followed the forestry rules of having so many buckets of water and dirt handy, whatever, and he got it put out with hardly any damage to anything but a piece of scorched earth where the tent had been."

"I'm beginning to see why your family calls you a disaster magnet."

"To this day, Spence will not let me be in charge of any fire-related thing. No barbecuing, no campfire, no lighting the Yule log in the hearth on Christmas Eve. It's embarrassing."

"You *are* a disaster."

"Don't I know it. You're going to hang up now, aren't you? You've changed your mind about me, about spending time with a big dope like me."

"Hey now, I don't think you're a dope."

It was his kindness that got her. His unending, constant kindness, even when he should be agreeing with her. Then it hit her. Duh. Could it be any more obvious? "Oh, no. I can't believe this. You have it, too."

"What do I have?"

"The flaw-blindness. Otherwise, you could see it."

"See what?"

He didn't know? That was only further proof. He was as fault-blind as she was. Unbelievable. "My faults? You can't see them, can you? All six hundred thousand of them."

"Nope. You look perfect to me."

"Then we're doomed. This is only a matter of time." She rolled her eyes, trying to make light of things. But that wasn't how she was feeling. Not at all. Suddenly it was so clear. His devotion, his kindness, his affection and his romantic gestures would last only as long as it took for him to realize the truth about her. "We might as well accept it now. One day you'll look at me and decide you can't take it anymore. Then the more-than-friends aspect of our relationship will be done. A great big crash and burn. Ka-blew-y."

"No crashing and burning. No ka-blew-y. I like you exactly the way you are, Ava. I like *who* you are. Or I wouldn't be inviting you to my birthday party either."

"What?"

"You know I'm turning thirty-one on Tuesday. I've finally talked my mom into just having a small family dinner at home. My grandparents are coming. I want you there, too."

This was such dangerous ground. This was like the camping trip. Everything was great and happy. Everything finally looked promising, like it really was going to work out. And when you stopped expecting it, when you were sure it was smooth sailing ahead, *that's* when disaster struck. Like a category five tornado touching down right where you're the most vulnerable.

But what did she say? This sounded like the next step—a serious step. "Did I hear you right? You want me to come to your birthday dinner?"

"I'm asking you, right?" Brice adjusted his Bluetooth headset before he slowed his truck to pull into the left hand turn lane at the red light. Rex was in the backseat, panting extra loud, as if he were in agreement. See how Ava improved their lives? Just talking to her lifted their spirits. "You'll come?"

"As long as I get to bring the cake."

"I'd love the dump truck cake."

"Anything else you want with it?"

"Nope. As long as you're there, what else could I want in this world?"

"Oh, you are totally Mr. Irresistible, aren't you? You keep saying things like that, and I'm going to have to start liking you."

"*Start* liking me?" Brice chuckled. "I thought you were already in that pond with both feet."

"You must be mistaken. I *hardly* like you at all."

He could just imagine her rolling her eyes, looking so sweet and sparkling, the way she did when she smiled. In his opinion, they were right in that pond with both feet together. It was scary, but nice. "I'll pick you up Tuesday at six-thirty—" His call waiting beeped. His mom. "Can I put you on hold for a few minutes?"

"Okey dokey."

Ava. She put a smile into his heart and made everything better. The sun in his eyes was brighter than he'd ever noticed. The greens of the lawns and trees in his neighborhood more vibrant. Greener than he'd ever remembered.

He hit the garage door opener and switched over to answer the call. "Hi, Mom."

"Brice? Is that really you, or just my imagination. I can't believe I'm not getting your voice mail. *Again.*"

Uh-oh. She didn't sound happy. He racked his brain but he couldn't think of a thing he'd done. "I've been busy finishing up a project."

"Yes, your father mentioned that. For that baker. That friend of Chloe's."

He pulled his truck into the garage, not missing the disapproving tone in his mother's voice. "Ava McKaslin is a friend of mine, too."

"I know Chloe did her a favor by letting us overpay her for that wedding cake."

"Mom, you can't fool me." He cut the truck's engine and swung open the door. "Ava didn't charge Chloe—or you—for that cake."

"And how do you know this?"

He opened the door and waited while Rex leaped out. "I'm bringing Ava to my birthday dinner, and she's bringing the cake. You're going to be nice to her, right?"

There was silence. Frosty silence.

This was actually going better than he'd expected. That had to be a good sign, right? He unlocked the inside door and held it for Rex, who was yawning hugely and lumbered lazily inside. "Mom?"

"I'm carefully weighing my words and there doesn't appear to be anything I can say that you would deem appropriate."

"You have until Tuesday to work on that." He

stepped around Rex who had collapsed in front of the nearest floor vent and opened the refrigerator. "I'm going to expect you to be on your best behavior."

"She's all wrong for you, you know that."

"It's not your decision who I date, Mom. Ava's important to me, and I want your word you'll be nice to her."

"I suppose I can try."

"Thank you. I'll call you and Dad later, okay? I've got her on the other line, so I need to go." He said goodbye, and he couldn't say exactly why there was a terrible sense of foreboding that settled dead center in his gut. He switched over to the waiting call. "Ava?"

"Yo. Danielle just walked in. She's taking the measurements for the shades she's making me. Hold on just a sec." There was a lot of cheerful talk in the background that grew fainter. "Brice? I've got a full house here. Spence just pulled up with the tables Aubrey refinished for me."

"Sounds exciting. I bet the place is looking more like you imagined."

"It is. I'm going to be officially open for business this weekend. There's a ton of stuff I still have do, and I'm totally excited *and* scared."

"I can understand that." Did he. "What can I do to help?"

"As if you haven't done enough with the wood-work. It still takes my breath away."

"Good. That's the idea."

Ava nearly stumbled at his words. Oh, she was so overwhelmed. So out of her realm of experience. Tender feelings for him just kept lifting through her, rising up until all she could feel was joy. Was it illusion? Could this possibly work out between them?

"I'll give you a call tomorrow," he said in that dependable, easy-going way of his. "See if you need any help hauling anything or helping with the set up. Okay?"

"Okay."

Ava leaned her forehead against the heel of her hand, listening to the click as he disconnected. Could this man be any more perfect?

It took her a second to realize that all the chatter in the front room had stopped. Her sisters were staring at her. Katherine's eyes were hopeful and sparkling. Aubrey looked as if she were going to start jumping up and down with glee.

This was another problem with a big family. A girl had no privacy. Ever. Even when you were grown and gone from the nest, you could not get away from nosy sisters, bless them.

Danielle shifted little Madison on to her other hip. "Did we hear that correctly? Are you going to a family birthday party?"

"Oh, this is *big*. Huge," Katherine added. "He's taking you home to meet his parents."

"See? What did I say?" Aubrey steepled her hands, as if in prayer. "This is the next step."

"Don't psych me out, I'm trying to cope here." Ava spotted Spence and his big gray pickup parked against the curb. He was glaring in at them. "He obviously needs help. I'd better get out there—"

"Was it my imagination or did you tell Brice about the camping trip?" Katherine asked, using the box Aubrey brought to prop open the door. "And he *still* asked you out?"

"The story just popped out. It wasn't intentional." Ava shrugged. "I guess that old family stuff has been on my mind lately."

"I know how that goes, but you don't have to let the past affect your future. Good things happen to good people, and this is one of those times." Katherine grabbed a pair of sunglasses from the counter. "Take my advice. Leave the past behind where it belongs, and go live your future. You can do that, right?"

"Sure." Easier said than done. She didn't dare let herself believe it. Being with Brice was too important. She hoped that as long as she stayed right here, in this more-than-friends-only stage, then it wouldn't get serious. She wouldn't lose any more of her heart.

Chapter Thirteen

On Tuesday evening, as they headed up to Brice's parents' house in his red sports car, she felt as if they were driving heavenward. The foothills of the Bridger Mountains offered breathless views of the higher Rocky Mountain peaks and the deep, divine blue of the summer sky. As gorgeous as the view was, where were her eyes glued? On Brice, looking amazing in a black sports coat, shirt, tie and trousers.

Dazzled? Yeah, you could say that.

"We're almost there." Brice drove with confidence on the smooth, S-curving road that skirted private developments more upscale than the one he lived in. "You look a little pale. Are you okay?"

Okay? If she could survive the panic attack, she'd be just fine, thanks. There was a perfectly rational explanation for the panic. This couldn't be real. It was too nice to be real. Too wonderful. She tried to relax. Tried to pretend she wasn't terrified. She'd never felt like this, so vulnerable and so close to him.

Careful, Ava, she warned herself. Don't start to believe in the dream.

Brice pulled into a grand driveway that rivaled anything she'd seen on TV and that's when the nerves hit her. What had she been thinking? It was way too early in their relationship for her to meet his parents. Besides, she'd already met his mom. She'd been very dismissive of Chloe's choice of wedding cake designs.

"I don't suppose your mom is expecting a more fancy cake design?" She looked at the bakery box sitting on her lap.

"Does it matter?" He shrugged as if he couldn't imagine how she might even think it would.

Okay, maybe not. But as he pulled in front of a lavish Shakespearean-looking brick home with a turret and those diamond panel windows, she couldn't fight the strong feeling that her nifty dump truck cake might seem a little hokey by comparison. "You're sure about the cake?"

"Yep." He didn't look like he had a doubt in the world.

Okey dokey. Maybe it wasn't the cake she was worried about. Maybe Brice's family would take one look at her and think, not right for him. She smoothed the linen skirt of the dress she'd borrowed from Aubrey.

Okay, really, it was just her old insecurities flaring up like a big case of emotional warts.

He smoothly parked the car in front of a four-car garage and cut the engine. "You haven't changed your mind about coming in with me, have you?"

"Let me get back to you on that." Her voice wobbled.

"Don't be nervous. My family is going to love you."

"And if they don't?"

"They will learn to love you." He cupped her chin in his palm.

She focused her violet-blue gaze on his, her whole heart showing.

He got out of the car, noticing his grandparent's Land Rover was parked in the shade. Anticipation uplifted him as he circled around to open Ava's door. He couldn't wait for his grandparents to meet Ava. He knew they would love her. His parents might take more time to accept someone new, but he knew they would come to adore her, too. How could anyone not fall in love with Ava?

He took the boxed cake and offered his hand to help her from the low-slung car. The brush of her hand to his renewed him, more every time.

Having her at his side was like a gift. She swept beside him with that buoyant walk of hers. Everything about her was bubbly. This evening, she wore a light purple summer dress that shimmered as soft as a dream. Matching lavender sandals clicked on the brick walk, echoing slightly in the balmy, quiet grounds. The purple gift bag she carried made a pleasant crinkling sound as she walked. Her hair was pulled back in one of those fancy braids and stayed in place thanks to a few little purple butterfly barrettes.

Cute. Whimsical. She was like a spring breeze and he could not get enough of her. Powerful affection filled him. He hesitated on the doorstep. "This is your last chance to bolt."

"How did you know that had crossed my mind?" She winked, and looked even more sweet and adorable. "I'm as ready as I'll ever be."

"Super-duper." He said that to make her smile, and it worked. He opened the front door. "Hello? Anyone home?"

Their steps echoed in a mammoth marble foyer.

Ava looked around, a little afraid to step on the very expensive looking marble beneath her shoes. "Is this a house or a museum?"

"It always felt like a museum when I was growing up. Come all the way in. Don't worry. We don't charge admission. Not on Tuesdays, anyway."

Her gaze went directly to an ornately framed watercolor, which was mounted on the wall directly ahead of her. It looked old. Ancient. Probably by some master—Aubrey would know which one. "That looks real."

"Mom likes to hang her expensive pieces where she can impress everyone who walks through the door."

"Me, too. We have a cross-stitch welcome sign hanging in our entry. Aubrey did it last winter. It's a total classic. We've had offers."

What was it about her that made even visiting his mother fun? He set the cake on the antique table against the wall.

"Did you really grow up here?"

There was that little furrow between her eyes again, a sign she was puzzled. So, he hoped, did she see what he wanted her to see? Most people who walked through the door were impressed by Monet and the imported marble. There were no family pictures framed and hung on the walls. No cross-stitched sign welcoming guests. No hints of love or comfort anywhere.

A maid in a black uniform hurried discreetly toward them. "Master Brice. Happy birthday! Let me take your things. The family is in the rec room. Dinner will be served promptly at seven."

"Thanks, Wilma. This is Ava. And here is the cake."

"Oh, well done. I'll get this to the kitchen." The tidy lady hurried off with efficient speed.

Ava knew she was gaping. Okay, call her intimidated now. What she had already seen of Brice's life was a neon sign they weren't compatible; *this* was a billboard framed in blinking red lights. "She took my purse and your gift."

"She's supposed to." Brice looked amused as he guided her through a cavernous formal living room filled with rich polished woods and upholstered velvet and toward a slowly downward winding staircase.

No way was this a *home*. It was too perfect to relax in, and there was no feeling of love or life. From the expensive imported carpets to the vase that looked like it came from ancient China. Where did his parents put up their feet at the end of a long day and watch television? And there wasn't a book anywhere. Not even a Bible. The rooms, stuffed with expensive furniture, felt vacant and hollow. There was no heart. No warmth.

This was Brice's childhood home? No way could she imagine children growing up here. Well, not the way she would want to raise children, anyway. With noise and friendly chaos.

Their footsteps echoed in the coved ceilings overhead, just like they would in a museum.

"Everyone's downstairs." Brice took her hand, his gaze and his touch were more than tender. It felt as if he cherished her. Being cherished by Brice Donovan was just about the best thing she could wish for, but with every step she took, she wondered how this could possibly last.

Voices grew in volume as they descended the grand staircase and arrived in a slightly less formal version of the living room. Four people rose from stiff, uncomfortable looking couches. Brice's parents and grandparents stopped in mid-conversation to stare at her.

During the few seconds of awkward silence, she felt Brice's hand tighten on hers. Tension rolled through her. The sudden silence felt uncomfortable. So did the hard way Brice's mother studied her.

Okay, she could see the mistake right away. She was wearing purple. Everyone else was dressed in sedate colors. Navy. Black. Beige. She stuck out like a grape Popsicle. Her dress wasn't floor length, her hair wasn't swept up and sedate. She wore her cross and not ten-thousand-dollar pearls—not that she had any or wanted to have any.

It was too late to rethink the wardrobe. The important question was whether Brice thought bringing her was a definite mistake?

"Everyone, this is Ava McKaslin," he said in that warm baritone of his.

Since her knees were a little wobbly, she took care stepping forward so she didn't trip as Brice introduced her to his parents.

"It's good to meet you." Brice's father, Roger, stuck out his hand.

She hoped her palm wasn't too damp. Oops. Nerves. She wanted her grip to be firm enough for him. She met his gaze, and she realized he had Brice's eyes. And they were warm and kind.

"I understand you designed our Chloe's wedding cake. That was beautiful. Everyone said so," Roger

Donovan said stiffly, as if he were uncomfortable, too. "Chloe comes back from her honeymoon tomorrow. I'm sure she will tell you herself how happy she was with it."

"Thanks. It's very nice to meet you." Her voice hardly wobbled at all. Whew. That went pretty well. Considering.

"And this is my mom, Lynn. I know you've already met."

Lynn Donovan nodded once, a curt bob that was barely an acknowledgement. "I understand you're designing Carly Frost's wedding cake. Maxime and her oldest daughter were just telling me today how pleased she is so far."

"That's nice to hear. I'm glad they're happy."

"Hmm." The woman managed to make that sound seem judgmental, and said nothing more. She pursed her lips and stared hard at Ava, as if she didn't like what she was seeing.

Okay, this wasn't going as well. Ava took a rattling breath, feeling more and more unsure. Until Brice's hand engulfed hers, and his touch was a steady anchor of comfort and reassurance.

"Hello, to both of you." His grandmother looked elegant in her designer pantsuit. She crossed the length of the room, arms out, and pulled him into a quick hug. "Happy birthday, young man."

"I'm glad you could make it." Brice kissed her cheek. "How was your flight home?"

"The usual. Lines. Customs. Only one lost piece

of luggage. An improvement from the trip over." Merriment twinkled in her eyes and she grasped Ava by the hands. "Ava, dear girl, how is your grandmother? Mary and I have been playing phone tag for the last few months."

"Gran is fine, or so I hear. I haven't spoken to her for the last few weeks, but she's scheduled to call soon. I'll tell her that you were asking after her."

"Tell her I demand she calls me."

"I'll tell her. It is good to see you again, Ann. And you, too, sir."

Brice couldn't believe it. He curled his hand around the nape of her neck, tenderly pulling her closer. "Okay, how do you know my grandparents?"

"We met at my Grandpop's funeral, although it's been a few years now," she explained. "I'm glad to see you are both well."

"As right as rain." Gram clasped her hands together as if in prayer. "How wonderful that you are with us here tonight, dear. To think you and Brice are dating."

"I'm afraid that's just a rumor. I suppose it will never stop if I keep hanging out with him."

"Oh, you have your grandmother's sense of humor." It was plain to see that Gram already adored Ava. "I hear you've brought the cake tonight. Something special for our Brice. Now, we'll know just how much she's fallen in love with him when the cake is unveiled. What fun."

"I'm afraid it's not what you're expecting." Ava rolled her eyes in that way he loved so much. "Brice requested the cake, so if you don't like it you have to blame him. I'm the completely innocent baker."

Ann and her husband Silas laughed pleasantly, as if they understood completely. Except for the fact that Brice's parents were staring at her as if she were their worst dream come true, the evening was going great.

The maid lady chose that moment to announce the salad was ready and to come to the table. She caught Lynn's coolly assessing gaze and thought, uh oh. But the minute his big hand enclosed over hers, she felt cherished all over again.

"See? They love you," he whispered in her ear.

She might not be so sure, but he looked happy and she wouldn't jeopardize that for anything.

"Did I tell you how beautiful you look?" he whispered again, hanging back to let the others head upstairs first.

"Not recently."

"On a scale of one to ten, you're a two hundred. A definite Miss Perfect."

Whatever you do, Ava, she warned herself, don't fall in love with him.

But it was too late.

Seated at his place at the mammoth dining room table, Brice couldn't believe how great dinner was going. Okay, Mom wasn't as warm to

Ava as he would have wished for, but she was doing pretty well considering. There had been no comments, bold or veiled, that could hurt Ava's feelings. It mattered to him that his mom was keeping her promise.

His dad, he could tell, thought she had it together. He'd quizzed Ava about her business plan, while Granddad had added his advice, and they both pronounced her plans financially sensible and well done.

Ava smiled in that sweet way of hers, winning his heart all over again, thanking Wilma as the maid cleared her plate.

Powerful love for her hit him like a punch to his chest. He couldn't breathe, couldn't feel his heart beating. He could see only her. Be aware of only her. Seconds stretched into eternity and it was scary, this all-consuming love for her. Scary, but right.

He knew she was the right woman for him. The real question was: Did she feel the same way about him?

"Excuse me," Ava said in her cheerful way, "but I'd better help set up the cake."

"Oh, the cake!" Gram clasped her hands together in anticipation. "This I have to see."

"I hope it's chocolate, like Chloe's wedding cake," Granddad commented.

His mother's lips pursed tight; but thank the Lord she kept her opinions to herself. Brice's heart swelled with love for his mom. He was proud of her. He knew how hard it was for her to keep her promise to him. Catching her gaze, he nodded his silent thanks, and some of the tension eased from around her mouth. He knew it was going to be okay.

"Yes, it's chocolate." Ava bounced up from her chair. "But this is a different recipe than I used with Chloe's cake. This is more like fudge. I call it my triple chocolate dream cake."

Granddad grinned. "I like the sound of that."

"He has a terrible sweet tooth." Gram shook her head, as if in great disapproval, but there was no mistaking the depth of love alight in her eyes. "What am I going to do with you, Silas?"

"Just love me for who I am, I guess," Granddad grinned at her.

Across the table, Brice recognized that loving glance his grandfather gave his grandmother and understood it for what it was truly, for the first time. Not merely love, but a breadth of love that happened to a man, if he was blessed, once in a lifetime. And he had to be brave enough to grab hold of that rare blessing and not let go, no matter how scary it was.

Opening himself up to love and hurt and rejection again was tough. But truly, Brice realized as Ava pushed in her chair, her purple skirt swirling, his heart had already made the choice.

Ava was his everything. He knew it, soul deep. He wanted to spend the rest of his life loving her, protecting her, cherishing her.

She took two steps and then turned to give him a death-ray glare. "From your chair, I think you can see part of the kitchen, and you are not supposed to see the cake until it's ready. No peeking. Got it?"

"Yes, ma'am."

"I see that twinkle in your eye. You're thinking about peeking."

"If I was, you've made me change my mind."

"Oh, *sure* I did." Was it so wrong that she wanted this to be a surprise? She'd worked really hard on his cake, just for him. She'd wanted him to be happy with it. As she headed to the kitchen, it occurred to her that making him happy was taking top priority on her list of the most important things in life, and how scary was that?

With every step she took through the magnificent house, she felt more and more out of place. Sure, his family had gone out of their way to extend their warmth to her, and she was grateful for that, but did that help all the bad feelings that kept wanting to bubble up like lava into a volcano's dome?

No. Not a bit. The pressure was building, and there was nothing she could do about it. She smiled at Wilma, who was busy setting down the cake plates in a totally fancy china pattern, and fetched the bakery box from its spot on the counter.

"Let me set out the cake," the maid lady said, as if possessive of her job.

"Oh, I want to make sure it's perfect. I'll just unbox it, then."

"Very well."

As Ava carefully picked up the box and moved

it out of Brice's sight, she felt the tangible stroke of his gaze like a tender caress to her cheek. Pure sweetness filled her heart, and she did her best to hold back every feeling. Every caring emotion. Every piece of growing affection she had for this man.

She stood frozen, his loving glance holding her in place like a tractor beam.

Don't let yourself fall any more in love with him, Ava. She gulped hard and forced her foot forward. It took a few more steps and then she was safely out of his sight. But out of the tractor-pull of his feelings?

Of course not. She felt the pressure building in the center of her chest, like the rising dome of that volcano about to blow. She felt little and plain and very purple in her dress, in this enormous kitchen that was roughly the size of her apartment. She could see into the next room—some kind of solarium thingy, with rich-looking imported carpets and antiques and more paintings on the walls— probably from some master she knew nothing about.

This was Brice's life, she realized. This was where he grew up, this was his childhood home, he'd had maids and probably nannies and, as she heard the conversation drift in from the dining room, he was intelligently discussing the summer symphony series.

She felt the first crack in her heart as she lifted

the lid of the box. Even so, there was no way to stop her love for him as it brightened in intensity. No way to hold it back. She didn't even know she could hold so much love inside her, but there it was, an infinite amount, welling up right along with the building pressure of the truth. The truth she could no longer deny.

Brice *was* Mr. Perfect. But not *her* Mr. Perfect.

The first stroke of agony burned like fiery lava licking at the edge of her heart. Who knew doom would fall so quietly? The only sounds were the muted clink of Wilma counting out the silver and gold-plated dessert forks and the pleasant murmur of voices discussing Beethoven from the next room.

All she had to do was to lean a little to the right, and she had a clear view of him. Of Brice, looking like a magazine cover model in his designer suit, the ivy league educated, successful son of one of the oldest and richest families in Montana. Mr. Eligible Bachelor, who looked comfortable in this museum of a house. This wasn't the Brice she'd come to know and, sadly, to love.

Ava felt another crack slice through her heart. She lifted the cake carefully onto the counter. She looked at it now through different eyes. She'd put her heart into doing her best job for Brice.

The big blue and red dump truck was parked in the middle of the cake board she'd decorated to look like a dirt and gravel road, made of sugar paste and crumbled chocolate cookies, tacked with sugar glue and sprinkled with edible gold sparkles, to jazz it up. A construction driver was tucked behind a steering wheel. D & M Construction was spelled out in silver script on the door. The bed of the truck was mounded high with gray boulders, which were individuals bites of iced cake.

Her best dump truck cake ever, and it didn't seem that way now. It wasn't right.

She wasn't right.

Brice's mother tapped into the kitchen and blinked, as if she were totally confused. "That's a cake?"

Yeah, just as she'd thought. Ava took a steadying breath and wished she was centered enough for a quick prayer, too, but she wasn't. "It's what Brice wanted."

"Yes, I can see that."

"I know, it looks really close to the real toy, doesn't it? But trust me, everything is edible."

"It's certainly…interesting." Lynn was apparently struggling for something complimentary to say.

But there was no denying the truth, not anymore. She lovingly slid the elegant white candle that had been laid out by Wilma into the center of the cab's roof. Just one candle, that was all, and it looked out of place on the cake.

She thought of the bright yellow number three and one candles she'd brought for the cake, and decided to leave them where they were—in the back of the bakery box. Lynn Donovan didn't look as if she'd ever used novelty candles. Only classy all the way.

Which was probably why the woman had such a pained look on her face. "Brice will be pleased with this, I'm sure," she said stiffly.

Ava caught sight of Brice through the archway, leaning to speak with his grandfather. Her heart cracked a third and final time. She'd been right all along. There was no way this could work.

"You see it too, don't you?" Lynn said quietly. "He's really a good man. He deserves the very best of everything, don't you agree?"

Yes. Her entire soul moved with that word. She wanted the best of everything for Brice, too. But the man she watched could have been a stranger. Sure, he looked like the Brice she'd fallen for, but the man she knew was a craftsman. He made beauty with wood with skill, discipline and heart. He loved fast-food nachos and drank strawberry milk. He had a sometimes well-behaved dog, an easygoing manner that made her feel comfortable with him, and a sense of humor that made her feel lighter than air.

But *this* Brice, he was the real thing, honest hard-working guy and the most eligible bachelor all wrapped up into one. He was so perfect, that was his flaw. She'd finally found it. She'd known all along this relationship couldn't work, didn't she? But did she listen to her experience, to that little voice inside her head, to the iron-clad no-man, no-date policy that was supposed to keep her from being hurt like this again?

No. She was foolish to think that there could be a Mr. Perfect for her. She always fell in love with the wrong men, and there was no man more wrong for her than Brice Donovan.

She was vaguely aware of Lynn ordering Wilma around, of being herded back to the table, of seeing the anticipation on Brice's handsome face as she slipped into her chair. But her mind was in a fog. Her heart was a total mess. Somehow she had to hold it together.

Ann gasped when Wilma entered, carrying the cake. "Oh, that's delightful. Simply *adorable.*"

Her praise felt like a blow from a boxer's glove, as kind as those words were. Ava swallowed hard against the lump rising in her throat. She had to hold down her negative thoughts and keep them from blowing over.

"That looks like the real toy," Silas said in wonder. "I can't believe that's a cake. Is it really a cake?"

"It's a real cake, Granddad," Brice spoke up. "And I bet everything on it is delicious."

"That's not real dirt, is it?" Lynn asked in distress.

"It's crumbled chocolate cookies," Ava explained gently.

His beautiful, precious Ava. He saw all the love she'd put into his birthday cake. The D&M Construction logo on the door. The dog seated beside the driver inside the little cab. The detailing that had to have taken hours. She'd done this for him.

One look at her and he was hooked like a fish on

a line. He loved her without condition, without end. She sat across from him, and the expanse of the table might separate them, but he could feel the connection of love strengthening between them.

"I've never seen anything like this," his dad said from the head of the table. "You have a talent, Ava."

"It's not hard at all. You'd be surprised how easy it can be. And fun, too."

"Can you make other things, besides trucks?" Granddad asked.

Ava bit her lip, looking as sweet as sugar icing. "Well, I just did a ballet shoe the other day. That was a first for me, but I've done all sorts of things. Everything from football cakes to a medieval castle."

"I'll ask for the medieval castle for my next birthday," Brice told her.

She beamed her beautiful smile at him, the one that gleamed like a little dream.

I'm in big trouble, he thought. Just when he'd thought he was so in love with her, he'd fallen as far as he could go, he fell a little more in love with her. As his dad started the first notes of "Happy Birthday" and everyone joined in, he didn't have to wonder what he would wish for: Ava.

She was his dream come true.

Chapter Fourteen

Brice pulled the car to a stop in a spot marked for visitors, in the shade of tall poplars that lined the grassy lawn of her apartment complex. Ava knew he was going to ask her what was wrong, and what was she going to say? That she'd done it again. It was all her fault. She'd brought this misery down on herself.

"Thanks for coming," he said, breaking the silence between them. "I hope my mom wasn't too much. She comes across a little sharp, but she's a softy down deep. My grandparents love you. I think you've got lifelong customers. Granddad wants to order a cake for his birthday next month. You might want to start thinking up something with a golf theme."

"I'll get right on it." Her voice sounded strained, but it was harder than she thought to hold back so much pain. The thing was, when you'd been struck by misfortune as much as she'd been, you learned to cope. There was that first initial hit that hurt deep, but then shock set in and it didn't hurt so much. You could figure out how to cope until the shock wore off. And she was just about there. She could feel the press of hot, sharp emotions slicing through the defensive layers of her heart. The burn of tears gathered in her throat, rising up, too.

"Why do you look so unhappy?" He studied her, leaning closer, his gaze tender with concern.

"I'm not unhappy." That was the truth, she told herself stubbornly. She wasn't unhappy; it was much, much worse. She'd known better, but here she was with the wrong man. And here she was, exactly where she tried to avoid being, clutching every shard of her broken wishes. Why had she done this to herself? She'd known from the start this would happen. She should have listened to the fears inside her heart and resisted his kindness and his charm and his affection.

Then again, how would she have resisted caring for Brice? He was perfect. A thousand on a scale of ten.

"Did something happen I don't know about? My mother was unkind to you." He said it as if he'd expected her to be.

"No, she was fine. The problem is all me. It's me. Just like it always is."

"How could that be possible? You're perfect to me."

His words were the final blow, echoing around

the damaged chambers of her heart. Agony clawed through her, so sharp and deep she squeezed her eyes shut against the physical tangible pain. How could a feeling hurt so much?

"Perfect? *That's* the problem. You just can't see it yet. You can't see me yet. And if tonight didn't do it, then I don't know what will."

"What are you talking about? Whatever it is, I can fix it. Just tell me."

Wouldn't you know it? She'd finally found a good man, a more-than-stellar man, and he was still the wrong man for her. How was he going to fix that? He couldn't see, yet, that this wouldn't work out. It couldn't. There was absolutely no way.

She was never going to be anyone other than someone who lost her keys, who liked the color purple, who liked cross-stitch on the wall instead of fine art. She didn't belong in his world.

She was doing them both a favor, cutting their losses now. Before they fell even more in love. Think how devastating that would be, right? Because every day she spent with him, she loved him more. So think what he would come to mean to her in a year. In two. How much more would it hurt her heart then, when it finally hit him that she wasn't the woman he'd made her out to be?

He deserved the right woman. The woman he thought she was. The woman he expected her to be. Since her vision was blurring, she released the seat belt while she could still see. The thunk of it sliding into place behind the seat hid the sob that caught in her throat.

"Are you crying?" Brice sounded distressed.

"Nope." If she could blink the tears away, then she *couldn't* be crying. Really. Even if the burning behind her eyes was getting worse.

"You look like you're crying."

"L-looks can be d-deceiving." She groped to find the door handle.

His hand caught her wrist, holding her in place. Why did the affection she felt in his touch feel like the final straw? The tears she'd held back so carefully leaked one by one down her face.

"Okay, I might not know what's going on," he said, "but this isn't right. Did I do something?"

She shook her head, more tears rolling down her face.

"Did I say something?" She shook her head again, leaving him at a total loss. He felt his chest crack with pain for her. "Ava, please tell me what's wrong. I can't fix it if I don't know what is broken."

"Oh, see how awesome you are?" She choked on a sob. "You just don't see it, do you? This just can't work. I mean, hello? I told you from the start. I'm a romantic disaster. I always pick the wrong man, and now there's you. What am I going to do about you?"

His thoughts were going in different directions, and his guts were telling him she was about to break up with him. It was his experience that women who were happy with you generally didn't sob like that.

He could feel her emotionally pushing him away, although she hadn't moved a muscle. "Wait a minute. I'm not the wrong man. Why are you saying that?"

"B-because it's the truth."

"It can't be the truth." Tenderness filled him, and a love so deep that it couldn't be measured. "Because I *know* this is right."

Did she have any idea all the vulnerability he saw in her big violet-blue eyes? That he could feel the worry and fears in her heart? That he could hear the unspoken agony she hadn't spoken aloud? He thought not, so he said it for her: "I love you. Just the way you are. I love that you forget your keys and know how to make a dump truck cake and that you always make the sunshine seem brighter, the world better, *my* world better."

She didn't answer. It didn't look as if she could, her hand at her throat, her eyes bright with emotion. He knew what she needed to hear. He knew he'd been holding back the truth in his heart, and now was the time to lay it on the line. He knew how much his reassurance meant to her. They were linked emotionally, spiritually; he'd known she was special to him from the beginning. She was heaven sent.

It was hard to find just the right words, so he went with what was in his heart. "I love you, Ava. This is the real thing. I'm very serious about you. You have to know that I'm in this forever. That one day, I'm going to get down on one knee and ask you to be my wife."

Her eyes widened in unmistakable fear. Fear. He hurt for her. Yeah, he understood exactly how that felt to be so terrified, but he was taking the risk. "This is the only way to get past the panic. You have to take that leap, Ava. You have to look at the man I am, and the promises I've made and have already kept and believe that I will be that man for you. Forever."

Her lower lip trembled. "See, that's what scared me. And if I'm this scared, it has to be a sign, right? That this is never going to work. Love ends, and I have to be smart about this."

"No, you're being scared. I can feel it, Ava. I can feel your heart, and right now, I'm sure in a way I've never been. Because I can feel how much you love me and how terrified you are."

"Yeah. I'm afraid for a reason. This is all wrong, and my heart is going to be totally devastated when you figure out that I'm just me. Just Ava."

"Just Ava? See, that's where you're wrong. You are my everything. My dream come true."

"*That* is why it can't work." She pulled away from him, when everything within him longed to draw her closer. Misery marked her face and shadowed her eyes. Sobs tore apart her words. "But this is better than you deciding down the road that I'm not what you want. That's what happened to my parents, you know. I watched it happen. I m-made it happen. Love isn't always enough."

"But—"

"No, don't say it." She stumbled out of the seat to get away from him, but he was saying it anyway.

"I want *you*, Ava."

She truly believed that he loved her. She only had to look at him to know that his love for her was deep. She felt so close to him she could sense his soul as if it were her own, and she could feel his love for her there, a love without measure.

But without end? That was the question. And she feared it had a different answer. If only she could peek into the future and know for sure, then she could find a way to think clearly past the fear overtaking her.

Love wasn't always enough.

That's why she did what she had to do. To be smart about this. To be logical. To hold it together. She could keep calm, hold her heart still, and keep her emotions frozen. She *would*. Really. She just had to make it as far as her apartment—she was almost there—and *then* she could fall apart. Into a hundred thousand tiny pieces, but not here. Not now. Not in front of Brice.

How did she put all that he meant to her in a few parting words? She was clueless. Panic blinded her. Fear gathered like a hurricane in her stomach. It felt like disaster striking one more time as she took a step away from the car. How could the action meant to save her from pain—to save them both from terrible pain—feel like the worst mistake ever?

Because you're afraid, Ava. She took another step back, not at all sure if she could keep going. What she knew for sure was that she could not reach out to him. The hurricane of fear in her stomach began to gust, like the edge of the storm hitting shore.

The plea in Brice's dark eyes, the sadness settling into his handsome face, the sincerity of his good soul, felt like the summer heat on her skin. It just went to show the power of this bond—at least on her side—and how much she stood to lose, to be hurt.

Walking away was the best choice. There would be no happily-ever-after ending for her. True love didn't exist for a girl like her. And if it did, would she take the chance to find out?

That made her step falter. There was Brice, climbing out of his car, coming for her. And she could feel his love for her—he was sincere. He did love her. But how did she tell him she was afraid it wasn't enough? That one day he would look at her and see a disappointment.

Lord, please help me, here. Show me that I'm doing the right thing. Please, I'm begging You. She took another step back, she'd chosen a direction and she had to stay on it. She needed the strong safety net of her faith, of her stable life, of the path she'd stepped off of when Brice had walked into her life.

Her cell chirped and vibrated in her little pocketbook. Saved by her family. The Lord worked in mysterious ways. She dug the phone out and flipped it open without even looking at the screen. She could feel that it was one of her sisters. Hopefully not calling to ask how the dinner with Brice's parents went.

"Ava?"

She didn't recognize the woman's thin and strained voice. She glanced at the caller screen. It was her stepsister's cell number. That couldn't be right, could it? The woman did not sound like Danielle.

"I—I'm so glad I caught you." Danielle choked out a sob. "Katherine's up hiking in the mountains with Jack, and she's out of range. Aubrey isn't picking up. I know you're probably in the middle of dessert or something, but c-can you come?"

"Absolutely." Ava felt her strength kick in. Now she knew why she'd felt as if doom was about to strike. "Come where? What's wrong?"

"It's *J-Jonas.* He's been sh-shot."

"Shot?" Shock washed through her. Jonas was shot? That didn't seem possible. She thought of her tall, kindly brother-in-law who always seemed so invincible. "You mean he was working tonight?"

"Y-yes. He's c-covering for someone on vacation, and—" Another sob broke her voice. "I'm at the hospital and there's no one to t-take the k-kids."

"I'll do it. Is Jonas going to be okay?"

"They d-don't kn-ow. Please c-come."

"I'm on my way." She snapped shut the phone. Okay, talk about a sign. There was Brice, watching her with concern in his eyes. So big and strong, everything within her ached for his strong arms around her. She longed for the safe harbor of his love.

How did she know that his promises were real? That she wasn't letting her fears rule her life? How did you know if a love would last? Well, she'd asked for the Lord to show her the way, and this was it. Her family was what mattered, the people she'd been able to love and trust all of her life. Not some romantic dream.

For a breathless moment their gazes met and she felt his empathy, his concern for her never wavering, steadily pulling her closer like a tractor beam.

How did she give in? How did she walk away? Panic crashed like a storm, stealing her breath, leaving her ice cold in the brazen heat. As afraid as she was to walk away and lose him forever, she was more terrified of really leaning on him. Of really trusting him.

"This is for the best," she said. "Family is everything. I think that when you love someone, you truly love them. That it's like the Bible says: *'Love never gives up, never loses faith, is always hopeful, and endures through every circumstance.'* That's not what I think we have."

She watched the pain fill his eyes, and she hated that she was hurting him. But it was for the best. It was the right thing to do. You couldn't go into a serious relationship already knowing it couldn't work.

And if that was her fear talking, then maybe that was for the best, too. Because how could a man as truly wonderful as Brice love her that way?

"Did you say that Jonas was shot?"

Somewhere in the dim recesses of her brain she remembered Danielle saying Jonas and Brice had volunteered together once. So it was only normal human concern behind his question. Somehow, she made her voice answer. "Yes. He was covering someone's shift tonight, I guess, and that's all I know. I promised my sister. I have to go."

"I'll drive you." He held out his hand, palm up, looking as valiant as a knight of legend, one of good deeds and of good heart and she was hopeless.

Never in her life had she wanted something so much as to place her hand in his. To throw caution to the wind and trust that everything would be fine. That he was right—twenty years down the road they would be together and happy. That they could survive the rift of his mother's disapproval, unlike her own parents could have done.

But it wasn't logical. It wasn't smart. It wasn't safe. She took another step back. It will only end in heartache, that little voice within her said. And if there was a part of her that knew she was really afraid, she couldn't listen to it. "I'll drive myself. I can't be with you. You are great, you have made such a difference in my life, but I think real love is like a special kind of heaven on earth. It shouldn't hurt like this. It just shouldn't be this frightening."

"Ava, wait. You wanted to know if this was the real thing, if we had a shot at a real happiness together. I'm pretty sure we do. But we'll never really know if you walk away. Don't you want to find out?"

"I already know." She hauled her key ring out of her purse and the first deepening rays of the setting sun brushed her with a rare magenta light, that shone like heaven's light. "Goodbye, Brice."

He couldn't say anything. He stood there like he was made of granite, despair filling him, watching her hurry the rest of the short distance to the covered parking. She slipped from his sight, and he felt the first fall of grief. The hard ball of it burned in his throat. Was he really losing her? How could she be so sure?

There was no way. Because he could see a different path. A different outcome. As intimidating as it was to be given this singular blessing of true love, he was more afraid of spending his life without her as his wife. Without her sparkle and her life and her brightness lighting the rest of his days.

He couldn't believe he'd lost her.

Chapter Fifteen

After saying about ten prayers for Jonas on the drive over, Ava couldn't keep thoughts of Brice away. He might be out of sight, but not totally from her mind. His words kept troubling her. *You wanted to know if this was the real thing, if we had a shot at a real happiness together. I'm pretty sure we do. But we'll never really know if you walk away.*

Hey, it wasn't her fault, she thought as she drove up to the parking garage and snapped a ticket out of the automatic dispenser. She dropped the ticket on the dash and waited for the red and white striped arm to lift. If her vision was blurring again, it was just from being so tired. Really.

Not because she felt as if there was an enormous void in the center of her ribcage, where her heart used to be. And as she pulled into the closest space by the doors and took the elevator to the main lobby, that void began to fill with bleak misery.

You did the right thing, she told herself as she took another bank of elevators to the intensive care floor. She wasn't going to set herself up for more doom. She wasn't the right girl for Brice. No matter how much she wanted to be.

As soon as the doors opened she popped out into the echoing corridor and headed down an endless hall with closed doors. She followed the directional signs, struggling to keep tight control of her feelings. She was here for Danielle, she was here for her family, where she belonged, where she was accepted, where she was safe.

Safe. That was the word that was haunting her. She felt the tangle of emotions ball up tight in her chest, growing tighter and tighter, sheer misery. Pain throbbed between her ribs, making it hard to breathe. Almost as if she were sobbing, which she wasn't, of course. Really.

She could do this, she could hold everything down, because if she didn't, she wasn't sure she was strong enough to hold back the tidal wave of sheer agony. How could she feel so alone without him? She'd been alone before, she'd managed just fine without Brice Donovan by her side. And if she needed him, then she'd learn to get past it.

Pain arched through her as if she'd broken a rib. It was only heartache. Although nothing like she'd ever known before. Because she'd never loved any man before the way she loved Brice. The way she still loved Brice. She didn't want to love him, she didn't think it was smart to love him. She didn't fit into his life, not really, and why start on a road you knew would end?

Okay, so she didn't *know* it would end. She was just terrified, but wasn't Brice right? If she could see through the blur of panic long enough to think clearly, she had to admit he was totally right. You didn't know unless you gave something a chance.

The truth? He terrified her. Absolutely. Positively. Without condition and without end. She was too chicken to hand over her heart to the one man who really wanted it. Because she was too terrified that he might get a really good look at her and stop loving her. That he'd see who she was deep down, at heart, at the bottom of her soul, he'd stop loving her.

Love ends, she knew it. Wasn't that the lesson of her childhood?

Yeah, that frustrating little voice inside her argued, but it's not the only lesson, right?

Right. She was afraid because she'd never been here before. Brice wasn't just Mr. Perfect, he was *her* Mr. Perfect. Exactly like a dream the angels had found in her heart and made real. She didn't have any reason at all to find fault with him and push him away. She was out of excuses. Out of options. Had she been picking boyfriends who weren't good enough so she didn't have to be right here, where it was so scary? Because the relationships had always ended, she'd be able to retreat back to her safe life, with her sisters and her lifelong job at the family bookstore. No risks. No failures. No pain.

Brice was different. That's why he made her feel all these things she hadn't had to experience before. Like being so vulnerable it was as if she were inching out onto a tiny little limb hanging way out over the Grand Canyon. With every move she could feel the limb sinking downward, getting ready to snap beneath her weight.

And like the scared little seven-year-old inside her, she'd jumped right off that limb onto the safe earth. Brice was right. If she stayed here, she would never know if the limb would break beneath her weight or if it would support her across the void.

Then she saw Danielle in the intensive care waiting room, her elbows on her knees, her face buried in her hands, sobbing, and Ava forgot everything but comforting her sister. Her heart broke at the strangled sound of Danielle's muffled sobs. As she came closer, she noticed a smaller room off to the side, where a volunteer was trying to read to the munchkins.

Tyler saw her first. "Aunt Ava! I wanna go home."

"That's why I'm here, cutie." As heavy as he was, she scooped him up and gave him a hard hug.

She didn't even want to think about what would happen to this little boy if his daddy wasn't okay. Madison was fussing in the volunteer's lap, a pleasant-looking grandmother type who had a sad smile as she put the book away and stood, taking care with the miserable little girl.

"You go help the nice lady with your sister, okay?" Ava set Tyler back down and smoothed his hair. "I gotta talk to your mom for a sec. Then we'll go by and get pepperoni pizza because you know that helps to make anything a little better."

Tyler nodded, swiped at his eyes with his sleeve and bravely went to help his sister like the good big brother that he was.

Ava's heart broke when she knelt down beside Danielle. She'd never seen her stepsister like this, her hair was tousled and her face streaked with tears. She simply wrapped her in a hug, feeling her heartache and terror. She couldn't bear to think about what Dani's future would be like without her beloved Jonas. With her great love lost.

Okay, she wasn't going to *take* that as a sign from above, because it wasn't. Really. She released Dani and fetched a full box of tissues, since the box on the table beside her was empty. "Any word?"

Dani shook her head. "He's still in surgery."

"That's gotta be good, right? He's hanging in there. And he has you and the kids to fight for. I've been praying on the way over. Do you want to pray together now? You'll feel better."

"Praying is all I've been doing. I feel terrible interrupting you tonight. Where's Brice?"

That was Dani, always thinking about everyone but herself. "Don't worry about that. I want to know what I can do for you. To make this easier for you."

"Oh, Ava." Dani wiped at more tears. "Nothing but Jonas being just fine is going to make me okay. Do you know what I've been thinking about? I can't get out of my mind how I complained at him this morning. How he wasn't home enough, he wasn't supporting me with the kids enough, that I didn't feel as if he were really listening to me about the hedges needing trimming, and I was so *mad* at him. Just mad. How stupid was that?"

At the misery on Dani's face, Ava's heart broke even more, impossibly, as if there was enough of it to break again. "I know you. You weren't that bad. You couldn't have been. You adore Jonas."

"I do. But if he passes away, then the last thing I said to him was selfish and unkind. And I was just tired, that was all, but it doesn't change what I said. That when I should have reached out to him, when I should have asked how he was feeling, why he was preoccupied, if there was something I could do for him, I pushed him away. And—" a sob tore through her words "—I just can't bear it."

"Shh, he knows how much you really love him. Dani, don't cry harder. We'll put it in prayer, all right?" She took her sister's hands, so cold, and cradled them in hers. *"Dear heavenly Father, please—"*

Even in prayer, she could feel Brice's presence, washing over her like a sign from above. *"—Please watch over Jonas in surgery and let him know that we love him, especially Dani, who is hurting so much. Please ease her worries, and bring Jonas back safe to us. In Your name, Amen."*

Like grace, peace washed through her. She opened her eyes to see Brice, with Madison cradled in one strong arm and Tyler's hand tucked trustingly in his much larger one.

He was such a good man. At heart. Of character. Decent to the core. Seeing him again made every vulnerable piece of her spirit long for his love. She wished she could go back and find the clue that would show her this relationship between them would have worked out right.

That was the real issue, wasn't it? That she was terrified that she wasn't enough. That any man— even one as sincere and incredible as Brice—could love her enough to weather any storm to come. She'd watched her parents' marriage crumble, and she never wanted to feel like that again. But how was the pain of not being able to love him, of not ever having the chance to be his wife, any better than never being able to love him at all?

"If it would help you out, I can take charge of the kids," he said. "Get them home and some dinner in them. Ava, I know you were going to do this, but no one else is here to be with Danielle. You should stay with her and let me do this for you."

Was she capable of speech like a normal person? No-oo. She just stared at him, falling in love with him all over again. Was it smart?

No. Was it sensible?

No. But could she stop it?

No.

The strength of her love for him overwhelmed her, filled with the blazing light of a hundred galaxies, so bright that it changed how she saw him. She now looked at him in a way she'd been too afraid of before. Through the eyes of her heart, through her deepest dreams and into her future. Where there was only a love for him so strong, that it felt as if nothing could defeat it. Nothing could break it.

She could see that happily-ever-after dream of hers, and it was within her reach. All she had to do was to accept it. She'd never realized how terrifying it was to be so vulnerable and to have a dream come true. It was so much to accept. So much to treasure. So much to lose.

So much to lose.

She understood better Danielle's agony. From a deeper place. Life was uncertain; anything or everything could change in a moment. She'd spent her life being afraid of that moment, of losing everything, that she'd lived her life to protect herself from what Danielle was feeling at this moment.

But was that how she wanted to live? To spend her years protecting her heart and her life from loss? How could there be any goodness in that? There would be no love and no joy. What if Brice was right? His words came back to her, and she knew, when their gazes met and held, that he was thinking this, too.

If she walked away now, she would never know. Maybe never knowing would be a greater sorrow than finding out what could ever be.

"Thanks, Brice. That would be great."

He didn't need to say anything, she knew he understood. They had things to say to one another, but not here. Not now.

"Let me give you my house key." She pulled her ring out of the pocket and removed the key with trembling fingers.

When she handed it to him, their fingers touched and peace filled the empty places in her soul. It was love, his love, that made her believe.

"Thank you," she whispered, because she had no voice.

"Anything for you, sunshine."

She believed him. She watched him walk away, remembering the Scripture she'd quoted to him. *Love never gives up, never loses faith, is always hopeful and endures through every circumstance.* It was all him, she realized. He was the man who embodied that verse. Who had a heart big enough and a character true enough to never give up, never lose faith and endure through everything.

And then, she realized, so did she.

"Brice is such a good man," Danielle said on a sob. "Sometimes you just don't realize exactly how blessed you are."

"And sometimes you do," Ava said, and knelt down to stick with her sister through the wait ahead.

Brice headed down the hallway, finished checking on the sleeping kids. Although it was nearly six in the morning, he'd been pretty much up all night. He hadn't been able to get a wink of sleep with so much on his mind. With so much left unsaid.

Ava had called around two in the morning to say that Jonas was out of surgery and was touch and go in intensive care. She would be by as soon as she could leave Danielle.

He'd just put the tea water on when he heard the front door creak open. Ava was in the entryway, dropping her purse and keys on the little table there. Exhaustion haunted her face and bruised the delicate skin beneath her eyes, but not outright grief. "He's doing better. Danielle's still with him.

"Good. I've been keeping him in prayer."

"Thank you." She moved aside, and it was hard to read what was in her eyes, what she intended to say, and then he knew why. They weren't alone.

Aubrey stepped in, holding a grocery bag. "Hi, Brice."

"Good morning. Would you two like some tea?"

"That would great, thanks." Ava answered for both of them, taking the sack from Aubrey. The twins exchanged glances and without a word Aubrey slipped down the hallway to check on the kids. Or, more likely, to give them some privacy.

Ava came toward him. "Katherine is at the hospital now, and we're taking turns with Danielle. It was really great of you to do this. It meant she didn't have to worry about her kids, and she wasn't alone until the rest of the family could get there."

"It was my pleasure." Brice came towards her and took the grocery sack from her arms and set it on the counter, so there was nothing between them. Nothing to hide behind. Only the truth of their feelings. "Do you know how devoted to you I am? How sure of my love for you?"

"I'm starting to get the picture."

He would always be devoted to her. Always ten thousand percent committed. Love moved through him of a strength and breadth that knew no bounds. That would never know a limit or an end. "Here is something you should know about me, something I haven't told you yet, but I intend to spend the rest of my life proving this to you. I will never give up on you. I will never lose faith in you. I will never fail you. Even if you ever give up on me, I will still be here. On your side. Come what may. I love you, Ava."

Her heart took a long tumble. Could he be any more wonderful? And wasn't that the scariest thing of all? Because right here standing before her, was every kind of heaven she could dream of having on this earth. Every blessing of love and faith and commitment she could ever wish for, and she would spend the rest of her life cherishing.

Totally scared, and yet more scared of not reaching for him, she pressed her hand to his, trapping the big curve of his palm against the side of her face. "I love you, Brice. Forever and ever."

"Then you'll marry me, when I get around to asking you properly?"

"Consider it a guarantee. You are my Mr. Wish Come True."

"And you, you are perfect for me, just the way you are, and that is never going to change. Can't you see that?" He looked so vulnerable for such a big man. All heart. All honesty. "You are the sun come into my life. I was in the dark before you."

He smiled. Not the dazzling one she'd so fallen for. Not the one that made his goodness of spirit show in his eyes. But a better one, a deeper one. One she'd never seen before. It was serious, too, and sincere, soul-deep.

He leaned closer and then closer still until his mouth slanted over hers. Slowly, his lips brushed hers with a brief, tender reverence. She was so in love all she saw was him. He filled her every sense and every thought. He was the reason for the beat of her heart now and forever. Her Mr. Wish Come True.

Epilogue

The first customer to officially walk through the newly opened bakery door looked very familiar. Ava squinted through the fall of light from the cheerful windows to the broad-shouldered handsome man closing the door behind him. Was he Mr. Perfect or what? Her soul sighed. She closed the cash register drawer, and her engagement diamond glinted in the bright sunshine.

"May I help you?" she asked courteously.

"I sure hope so." Brice Donovan carried a vase of yellow and red rosebuds and placed them on the counter between them. "I've come to check on the progress of my cake."

"Lucky for you, Mr. Wonderful, I just finished boxing up your order."

"Say, you wouldn't want to go get a cup of coffee afterward all this, would you?"

Call her happy. Why wouldn't she be? She was engaged to the best man in the entire world. Okay, she might be just a little biased when it came to Brice, but only a tad, a dash, a smidgeon. "I'll have you know that I'm engaged to be married."

"Lucky guy."

"No, lucky me."

His kiss was the sweetest heaven. The way his love filled her was the best of blessings.

The bell on the door chimed, and more customers tumbled in. Aubrey and Katherine, dressed for work at the bookstore. "It's a little quiet in here," Aubrey said.

Katherine took a look at the two who'd quickly stepped apart and smiled. "And for a good reason. Ava, after you finish my wedding cake, you'd better start on your own."

"I know." They hadn't set a date yet, with Jonas still recovering in the hospital, but they weren't in a serious hurry. They had the rest of their lives together. How amazing was that? "Wait, does this mean you've decided on a design for your wedding cake?"

"Yes. Finally." Katherine beamed her own happiness.

Wasn't this a wonderful world? Okay, so it wasn't perfect, but look at the blessings the Lord gave every day. Love and families and sisters. Hope, dreams to come true and chocolate cake. Lots of chocolate cake.

"The climbing roses design, right? I knew it." Ava rolled her eyes. The door chime rang again.

More customers? Then she recognized Brice's grandmother, Ann, and his mother, Lynn, who was *almost* actually smiling.

"We thought we'd stop by and support your business," Ann explained, pausing to press a kiss to Brice's cheek. "And to pick up some treats for our garden club meeting this afternoon."

"You came to the right place." Delighted, Ava went to box up a chocolate dream cake, only to have Aubrey step in to do it.

"Go," her twin shooed her away. "Mr. Perfect needs you. I can help out until the teenager gets here."

"Cool. Thanks, Aub." Did she mention what a great blessings sister were? They were absolutely wonderful.

"Come with me," Brice said, taking her by the hand and pulling her into the kitchen. He wanted a moment with her all to himself. He waited until the door swung closed and they were alone before he pulled her into his embrace. It was a long day and would probably be a busy one, and he wanted to say this while he had the chance. "I'm proud of you, sunshine. You know how much I love you, right?"

"Sure, but a girl always likes to hear it on a daily basis."

"I do love you." He cradled her face with his hands, sheer tenderness.

She kissed him sweetly, so happy she was floating like a big helium balloon, but this time there was no doom in sight. How could there be?

They were in this together, a team. Between the two of them and with the Lord's help, they could solve any problems that came their way.

"I love you, too," she told him, this man who was her idea of heaven in this imperfect world, and would always be.

Wow, was she turning into an optimist or what?

With joy in her heart, she thanked the good Lord before giving her husband-to-be another sweet kiss.

* * * * *

Don't miss Jillian Hart's next
inspirational romance
EVERYDAY BLESSINGS,
available June 2007.

Dear Reader,

Thank you so much for choosing *Every Kind of Heaven*. I hope you enjoyed Ava's story as much as I did writing it. Ava has learned to expect doom—she's dated a few too many less-than-stellar men. But when Brice walks into her life, his steadfast goodness and caring make her rise to the challenge of changing her view of herself and embracing the heavenly blessing of true love in her life. I hope Ava's story reminds you of how gracious God is and the wonderful gifts He sends into our lives with every day.

Wishing you heavenly blessings,

Jillian Hart

QUESTIONS FOR DISCUSSION

1. At the beginning of the book, Ava believes that the kind of man she needs, one perfect in every way, does not exist. What's a nice girl to do? Settle for Mr. So-so or Marginally Moral? Have you ever felt this way? What does it say about Ava's character that she refuses to settle for Mr. So-so?

2. What is Ava's first impression of Brice? How does her impression of him change after learning his real identity? How does this change her feelings toward him?

3. Brice is charmed by Ava's insults, when other men might be offended. Why isn't he offended? What does this say about his character?

4. Why is Brice truly the most eligible bachelor? What traits make him a good man?

5. What real fears are behind Ava's no-men, no-dating policy? Why does Ava look at Brice and decide only romantic disaster awaits her if she dates him? How does Brice convince Ava to amend her no-dating policy

6. As Ava and Brice get to know each other more, what aspects of their character does each come to admire?

7. What does the work that Brice does for Ava represent?

8. Why is Ava the perfect woman for Brice? Why is he the perfect man for her?

9. Ava's mother abandoned her family when Ava was seven years old. How does that affect her? How does that keep her from trusting others? What pattern is she afraid of repeating by falling in love with Brice?

10. How important are the values of family to Ava? How does her family help her through the hardships in life? How important are those values to Brice? How does this influence their growing relationship?

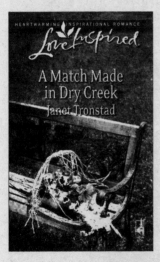

Celebrate Love Inspired's 10th anniversary
with top authors and great stories all year long!

Love Inspired®
SUSPENSE
RIVETING INSPIRATIONAL ROMANCE

From bestselling author Lyn Cote
comes the brand-new miniseries

The calm surface of this
Lake Superior community
hides dangerous secrets...

DANGEROUS SEASON
Available April

DANGEROUS GAME Available May
DANGEROUS SECRETS Available July

Steeple
Hill®

www.SteepleHill.com

LISHILC

REQUEST YOUR FREE BOOKS!

2 FREE INSPIRATIONAL NOVELS
PLUS 2
FREE
MYSTERY GIFTS

Love Inspired®

YES! Please send me 2 FREE Love Inspired® novels and my 2 FREE mystery gifts. After receiving them, if I don't wish to receive any more books, I can return the shipping statement marked "cancel." If I don't cancel, I will receive 4 brand-new novels every month and be billed just $3.99 per book in the U.S., or $4.74 per book in Canada, plus 25¢ shipping and handling per book and applicable taxes, if any*. That's a savings of 20% off the cover price! I understand that accepting the 2 free books and gifts places me under no obligation to buy anything. I can always return a shipment and cancel at any time. Even if I never buy another book from Steeple Hill, the two free books and gifts are mine to keep forever.

113 IDN EF26 313 IDN EF27

Name _____ (PLEASE PRINT) _____

Address _____ Apt. # _____

City _____ State/Prov. _____ Zip/Postal Code _____

Signature (if under 18, a parent or guardian must sign)

Order online at www.LoveInspiredBooks.com

Or mail to Steeple Hill Reader Service™:

IN U.S.A.: P.O. Box 1867, Buffalo, NY 14240-1867
IN CANADA: P.O. Box 609, Fort Erie, Ontario L2A 5X3

Not valid to current Love Inspired subscribers.

Want to try two free books from another series?
Call 1-800-873-8635 or visit www.morefreebooks.com

* Terms and prices subject to change without notice. NY residents add applicable sales tax. Canadian residents will be charged applicable provincial taxes and GST. This offer is limited to one order per household. All orders subject to approval. Credit or debit balances in a customer's account(s) may be offset by any other outstanding balance owed by or to the customer. Please allow 4 to 6 weeks for delivery.

Your Privacy: Steeple Hill is committed to protecting your privacy. Our Privacy Policy is available online at www.eHarlequin.com or upon request from the Reader Service. From time to time we make our lists of customers available to reputable firms who may have a product or service of interest to you. If you would prefer we not share your name and address, please check here. ☐

LIREG07